Memoirs of Pa... Pentecostal Private Eye

Written & Illustrated by Jeffrey Cortez
Editor- Meagan Rose Cortez

Story & Illustrations Copyright 2023 © All Rights Reserved

Dedicated to Mary Ann Durden Cortez
My Irish-Native American Porcelain Doll

On 1984 my Mary Ann left Florida, the land of her upbringing, to accompany me in The Boogie Down South Bronx, the land of my upbringing. She was not dissuaded by urban pastor wives and church friends that betted she wouldn't last long in what they held to be an urban wasteland. I now shamelessly admit enjoying observing many machismo egos become rattled and visibly defensive by her straight up frankness. Mary loves God and Bronxites hard, fully diving in for decades without hesitation to serve in Jesus' Name in intimidating places many folk thought she wouldn't last a week. She instilled in our three daughters a powerful non-showcase love for The Lord, others, fairness and education. She has been a prayer filled Lioness protective of me and a kindred spirit encourager in our following a path not paved with peer pressured stones. (Now, to make our children, grandkids, family members and church family cringe or blush) Mary also has been and continues to be, my steamy hot lover akin to how the book of Song of Solomon (according to some bible scholars) describes the love between the Lord and His Church Bride, whom He longs to return for.

Table of Content

Some Unsolicited Reviews

"Reading your novel had me reminiscing about my own struggles pastoring a small challenging storefront congregation. But I would never exchange them for anything else in the well paid universe." -Dr. Solomon Ojo De Águila-

"A rather borderline upsetting, irreverently critical and yet humbling mention of our underground praying community. Nevertheless as salt of the earth, we take the main character's perspective with a grain of salt and strive to do better"
-Orad Sin Cesar Society, Inc.-

"Thank you for boldly and respectfully reminding us fellow pentecostals, without diminishing the supernatural gifts of the spirit, that speaking in tongues is Pentecost in diapers" -Pastora Sylvia Yatusabes-

"An unauthorized exposé of unethical practices that some religious institutions have adopted, tragically exchanging God's power for silver and gold."
-Eva Marx de Cristo, Reformed Street Activist-

"Memoirs of Pastor Rajatabla - Pentecostal Private Eye made me angry, cry and laugh. I'm learning to love hating this author."
-Dra. Dominique Recta-

Preface

Greetings from the South Bronx, New York City, where at the age of five years old, over sixty years ago, I was introduced to my Spanish Pentecostal adventure. I wrote this fictional work with mixed emotions and a supersized side order of gratitude. These logged short stories were inspired and drawn out from vintage circulated Spanish Pentecostal urban legends, actual experiences shared by belated mentors during my relatively expensive formal pastoral education, my own personal ministerial experiences and love for storytelling. This makeshift quirky novel is meant to be both borderline irreverent and lovingly embracing of what the Lord has allowed me to be tested through and enriched by. I hope and pray that it would be of some sort of therapeutic processing aid to those that have survived any toxic versions of Pentecostalism as well as being uplifting to those called to tirelessly serve others through this 'movimiento de Dios' (movement of God).....whether it be in its classical modality or guised in nondenominational garbs :)

Con Mucho Cariño (with much affection),
Jeff AKA PJeff AKA Rev. Jeffrey Cortez LMSW

Introducing Pastor Rajatabla

Raja was born in New York City and raised in a strict Spanish Pentecostal household. His first learned language in his home as a child was Spanish and later learned English when he began to attend public school as a kindergartener. He spent a couple of years of his adolescence in Puerto Rico and had to become reacquainted with English when he returned to live in the Bronx, New York City. Although born Solomon Ojo De Águila , he was given his Raja nickname by his parents and church community as a side joke referring to the Spanish term 'rajatabla'. Rajatabla is a Spanish jargon indicating the rigorous actions of following orders or instructions exactly and strictly to the letter. In religious circles, it is usually applied to folks who attempt to practice portions of scriptures in a completely literal manner, but not necessarily considering their written context. As he grew older, he became aloof to believing in God. He later prayed for God to please place belief in his cynical heart if He really existed. Miraculously, his prayer was answered during a very dull evening church service. He was filled with a passion for following God's prompting. A couple of seniors told him that they had dreams of Pentecost tongues of fire flaming over Raja's head, similar to those documented in the Bible. Now he pastors a challenging and financially struggling small storefront church in a large metropolitan city. Raja is a bi-vocational clergyman, financially supporting his family and ministry with a secular job. He grew a low key reputation, within a religious dogmatic subculture inside Spanish Pentecostal circles, of his being able to dicipher mysteries within hysteria, gossip and sincere concerns. Church members, fellow clergy and members of other congregations usually seek assistance from Pastor Raja concerning these mysteries. He is far from being a mindless adherent to the letter of gossip, but rather a rajatabla stickler about seeking out the ignored context of unsettling mysteries informally commissioned for him to solve. Aside from Raja not being assumptive of details presented to him, how he goes about to solve mysteries is at times unsettling to the folks bringing him these cases. In his diary he logs issues presented to him as well as their discovered outcomes, which at times are hilarious and at other times somber. Raja has tongue in cheek nicknamed his memoir journal Tabla.

More Than Pigeon Feeding

"Do not rebuke an older man harshly, but exhort him as if he were your father...." (1Tim 5:1a NIV)

Sister Bienvenida called Raja and informed him of her concern about an elderly couple at her church. Raja would have politely told her that it was very late, he was tired from a long work day, but shied away from asking her to call the next day. Now this particular late-night caller had pioneered and founded a well-known large Pentecostal church. She did this at a time where there was much strong opposition to Pentecostalism by local society and historical churches. For decades, she mentored well-known missionaries, evangelists and church planters. In the past, Raja himself had the privilege to sit in her Tuesday night prayer/ bible studies. She spoke of her first-hand experiences of being harassed and insulted in front of her storefront church. One amazing story she told was of incidences where people threw vegetables at her and her bible students during street meetings. She then collected the thrown produce and later made delicious stews out of the unkind contributions. It was rumored that once a week Sister Bienvenida would purposely go to a farmers market in the Bronx Little Italy area where she, was also veggie assaulted. These would end up being be a source of large pots of stew cooked for a soup kitchen ministry she founded.

Anyways, Bienvenida suspected that an elderly newlywed husband, Brother Paco, from her church was suicidal. A former church member who lived next door to Paco and wife Juanita had 'overheard' a disturbing conversation and conveyed it to Bienvenida. This reportedly was then communicated to the couple's young pastor, Rev. Nico, who in turned reportedly became annoyed and dismissed the urgency of having an intervention conducted. As per other church members, the elderly pair hadn't been attending religious services for a couple of weeks. Raja added this mystery to a list of items he would pray about, seeking the Lord's guidance. One afternoon, Raja was enjoying a window shopping walk downtown on one of his mental health days. He stopped momentarily by a Victoria's Secret store looking at their window display and humorously pondering what to get his supportive wife, Tesoro, for Valentine's Day. An older couple came out from the store and immediately recognized him, calling him by name. Embarrassed, he greeted them and apologized for not remembering them. They did not know him personally and just remembered him as a guest speaker at their church some time ago. They introduced themselves as Paco and Juanita. It turned out they had decided to reserve a midtown hotel room a couple of weeks ago to enjoy the city's free events and delicious soup kitchens as a secret getaway extended honeymoon. They giggled as Raja told them about their community's concerns over their absence. Paco and Juanita then filled in essential details.

Dear Tabla-

The newly married couple, Paco and Juanita, fed birds as one of the activities their young pastor strongly recommended instead of making love. Previously, during their pastoral premarital counseling, it was found out that the male senior had a very serious heart condition. Their pastor warned them that if Paco had sex, he would most certainly die. So after a wonderful wedding, they had the daily routine of eating three simple healthy meals, listening to soft music, feeding birds in the park and each going to their separate bedrooms at night. This went on for two weeks. One night there was a knock on Juanita's bedroom door. She quickly put on her night robe and asked Paco what he wanted. He answered 'Me quiero morir...' (I want to die). That night, ignoring their pastor's warning, was full of ecstatic hallelujahs as well as other miraculous nights, mornings and afternoons. Thank goodness the ill-informed pastoral guidance they received didn't fully kick in. As I related my findings to Elder Bienvenida and the couple's young pastor Rev. Nico, they were at first stoic, then laughed hysterically. They agreed to keep lines of communication open. The pastor conceded that he needed to be less dogmatic and ignorant when counseling aging congregants. Bienvenida interjected "Especially married horny ones".

The Lord Squeezes But Doesn't Strangle

"Show your fear of God by not taking advantage of each other. I am the LORD your God."
(Leviticus 25:17)

Raja and his wife Tesoro at times would discuss and encourage each other on their ministerial choice of purposely pastoring a small congregation. Often, these tiny storefront churches weren't financially sustainable to hire full-time clergy nor even pay the lease. At times, Raja was approached by board members of large well-to-do churches and offered a full-time lead pastor position with attractive benefits. Presbyter Santos approached Raja seeking assistance in locating a missing pastoral family from a nearby fast growing church fellowship. The congregation had been very confused, especially when learning that their Pastor Saul had reappeared as a hospitalized patient with his family nowhere to be found. Missing persons flyers were being made and spread around neighborhoods with Raja's phone number (without his consent). Late one evening, Raja received a phone call from the missing wife's brother (the hospitalized pastor's brother-in-law). It turned out that Pastor Saul was hospitalized in the mental center and unit floor where Raja had worked as a psychiatric social worker.

Dear Tabla-

I used my credentials to enter the hospital's psychiatric ward and compassionately confronted mental health inpatient Pastor Saul. He had intentionally admitted himself as a suicidal person as a ploy to get sympathy from church members and locate his family. The man had been abusing substances and his wife. The dangerously mistreated wife ran off with the kids to another state into a shelter for victims of domestic violence. Pastor Saul (not his real name) and his wife, a couple of years earlier, came to our home to invite us to be co-pastors. Although an attractive offer with a nice financial income, we respectfully declined because our hearts were to pursue serving families impacted by substance abuse and domestic violence. Little did Tesoro and I know how prophetic this moment was. It was not the first time nor last time we would in retrospect realize how things we have said in an effort to counsel or engage in innocent conversation would be prophetic opportunities for friends to turn away from tragic events. So there I was with a surprised wide-eyed Saul in a psych ward where I had previously worked as an assistant psychiatric social worker. Saul offered me his church, which I'm sure had insidious strings attached. I informed him that I was never interested in ministerial political self- promotional moves, but mostly cared about the flock. His flock was now very confused and overwhelmed. I shared my plan under much prayer, encouraged him to focus on his total non-rushed recovery and that I would give the church members safe passage to other healthy fellowships. It was hard to do, but who was I to disobey the burning lead of the Lord who has always kept me safe in the eyes of storms? Some of my friends jokingly call me The Lord's Stealth Darth Vader. I'm not thrilled with the title, but at times it makes me laugh. How did Saul react? What could he do? Looks like although he was acting crazy like a sly fox, the True Shepherd had him in a tight straitjacket. Like the old Spanish adage goes, "El Señor aprieta pero no ahoga" (The Lord squeezes but doesn't strangle).

Canta Petros Canta

"You are altogether beautiful, my darling,
And there is no blemish in you"
(Song of Solomon 4:7)

Rafaela was a devoted music lover and rumored to be a notorious nymphomaniac who had married a much loved humble man in the church community. There was much suspicion, garbed in churchy gossip, that the Jezebel philanderer had wooed modest Petros with an ulterior motive to have access to his enormous savings. The less flattering reason was restlessly based on the scandalmongering question of why would such a very beautiful woman, known only to pursue handsome men, marry a quite homely man. After sharing these concerns with Tesoro, she agreed that it would be better that she, instead of Raja, approach Rafaela regarding these unflattering 'bochinche'.

Dear Tabla-
My better half Tesoro came back from investing in a overpriced Starbucks breakfast date with Rafaela. Tesoro came back with a funny yet touching report. There were many churches that would not allow males and females to sit next to each other in their sanctuary unless they were married. Pews were separated by gender, usually with a walk through aisle straight in the middle as a chasm. When visiting churches, Rafaela would avoid the ones with such pew arrangements. Or she would sit at the end of the aisle where she could scope out the male herd. Rafaela was tired of years of church hopping, man hunting and sampling church beefcakes only to have relationships end miserably. One night she walked into a small storefront church she had never been in before. She vowed to God that she would make that small church her permanent church fellowship, outlive her seductress label and would marry the man who would sit on the empty wooden foldup seat next to her that very night. As soon as she made that pact with God, the ugliest man she ever saw sat next to her. With a faint trembling voice, she told the Lord that she would

still keep her promise. The man turned out to be a guest gospel singer with the most beautiful voice Rafaela ever heard. Rafaela and Petros married. Some nights while in bed she would wake up, look at Petros and feel horrified at how homely by worldly standards he was. Then she would briefly turn over and say to her precious spouse, 'Canta Petros Canta' (Sing Petros Sing). Then, just like the Psalmist David's harp would relieve King Saul of his vicious mood, Rafaela's own ungrateful perception would be divinely readjusted....'Canta Petros Canta' ...

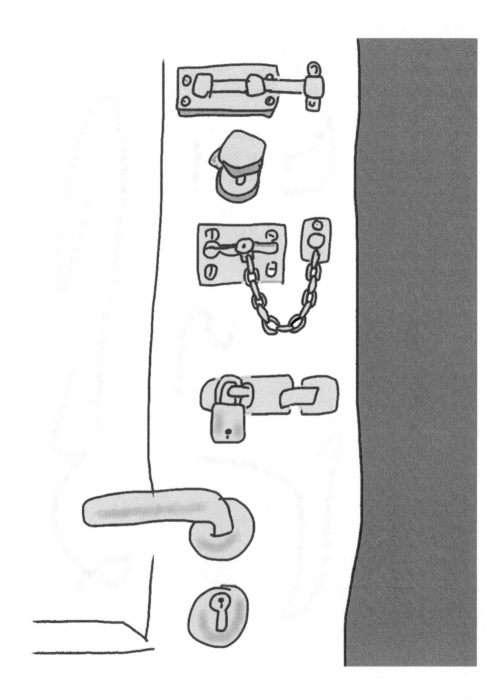

Delivering Bobo

"God is our refuge and strength, an ever-present help in trouble" (Psalm 46:1)

Raja remembered Fuego Avila from the time when he as a visiting "chaplain", totally ignored the residential's set protocols for visiting speakers regarding how to speak to an audience dealing with two hundred men with mental health issues. To be careful with metaphors and allegories which the men may dangerously take literal. Avila used a dynamic tone and volume during his sermon and repeatedly talked about power and fire. One of the men later fixated on the visiting speaker's charisma and keywords. Later in the evening went down and set fire to the basement of the residential building. Thank the merciful Lord, the fire was stopped in the nick of time. The well-meaning yet dismissive speaker was banned from ever coming to the facilities to "minister the word". Years later, Raja was invited by a now known loud street preacher, Megaphone Avila, to pray over a young man named Bobo. Bobo's mother was at her wit's end and had brought the son requesting healing. Avila 'discerned' that the young man was possessed of several spirits, including autism, low intelligence, mutism, etc , etc, ETCETERA SHANDA!!!!! Raja often prayed in private that God would help him navigate through things not cut and dry, things in the realms of gray areas. Raja prayed a compassionate prayer requesting deliverance from society's ignorance. Bobo's face brightened up.

Dear Tabla-
So yesterday, after Sunday church service as I was pulling down the front gates of our storefront church, Bobo approached me with a mega-sized Bible under his arm. He engaged me in Spanish with a greeting and asked: "May I bother you with a question?" I humored him and then he proceeded "Which animal did Moses not allowed into the ark?". After a

few seconds and really wanting just to go home and lay down for a nap I conceded that I did not know. Then the young man inquired "Really, you don't know?". Then I retorted that it wasn't Moses that led the animals into the ark, it was God. Then the young man replied "Moses wasn't there. It was Noah", then he strutted away. I walked home joyfully laughing at myself for that miraculous sucker punch. Sadly imagine person's potentials being oppressed by mislabeling their situations as a consequence to their behaviors or supposed limitations as evil oppression. During my way home I remembered a mentor, Hermano José García, who modeled compassion for me during rough patches in my young life. So when I got home I started writing my first social media based article.

The Sunday School Teacher That Saved My Life

I was 12 years old when I walked back home from school a month or two shy from the summer of 1969. Mom was not answering the door. Once my stepfather got there he opened the door, entered and then rushed out for the ambulance. In my desperation I knocked on the door of my neighbor...the last of the Caucasian Baptist pastors in the Bronx. He came into our apartment to my parent's unhappy bedroom. My grandmother was nearby doing door to door evangelism and felt led to come by and visit that afternoon. I remember her rushing in. I overheard from the adults that my mom had consumed toxic liquids to end her life. Mami had been trying that for a long time. I would often remove steak knives and razor blades from under her pillows. Once I caught her trying to drink Clorox. Pouring an extra glass she asked if I wanted to join her...I smelled the glass. I asked her if we would go to heaven if we did this. She put away the glasses and Clorox bottle and told me God had better things in store for us.

Now here she is laying on her bleak bed with her eyes rolling back and foam bubbling out of her mouth. She was dying and my little brother and I were crying and screaming. The pastor looked up toward our cracked ceiling to pray out loud and my grieving grandmother pulled out of her missionary giant carry bag and poured her anointing oil (Aciete de Oliva...Olive Oil) out of her Goya bottle and into mom's throat. Finally I got to see Baptists and Pentecostals working together. The 'worldly cigarette smoking' clergy was asking God for Divine intervention. I threw myself onto the floor into a prayer tantrum. Mami was taken away by ambulance to the old Lincoln hospital.

A couple of hours later my younger brother and I were outside in the street being comforted by our older cousins when we saw our grandmother return from the hospital slurring that her daughter had died. Grandmother was sedated and talking erroneously. Mom was not dead...but I didn't know that. We went to the hospital emergency room where we were met by church members. With the Devil's rage many of them pointed their fingers, blaming me for mom's suicidal ideations and attempt. I was the disgusting murderer. Out of nowhere my angel appeared. His name is Hermano José García. He was the Sunday School teacher that graciously taught me about the Lord. I was one of his rowdy smart mouthed Sunday school brats. In the chaotic emergency room he stood between me and my accusers. Jose boldly told them that it was not my fault and that my mom was just mentally sick. He gently and assertively took charge and asked my stepfather for the house keys and escorted me away from my adversaries. He assured me that it was not my fault and that my mother was just sick. When we arrived to my apartment door, poor Brother García had to figure out which combination of the several locks to try open up. Throughout this door/vault-like puzzle he assured me that it was not my fault and that my mother was just sick. I took some clothing and he made sure that I had taken what I would appropriately need for the remainder of the week. He walked me over from Cypress Avenue several long street blocks to Brook Avenue where my abuelita lived, all the way there he was assuring me that it was not my fault and that my mother was just sick.

The doctors didn't understand how the pipe drain cleaner didn't burn out my mother's insides...they would rather attribute it to the phenomenon of divine intervention than to just some local bodega store purchased olive oil. These physicians were less science fiction theorist and more theists I guess. After medical observations and treatments my mother was discharged to Bronx State Psychiatric where she spent much of the summer in therapy. I spent much of that summer zoning out and staring at walls, trying to micro detail out how I could have prevented my mother's hate of life. In my fog I often would see and hear my accusers. But my sanity's guardian angel would appear in my mind...I could hear his voice...assuring me that it was not my fault and that my mother was just sick. In a church bogged down with stone throwing cultural dogmas and guarded socio-emotional dysfunctions God sent me someone not arrogantly bound to Bibliolatry but to Christ-like life changing compassion. He was there years later to guide me through my post born-again liberal outbursts into safe places of maturity. Recently I found Brother Jose through one of his in-laws in FaceBook. I'm frustrated in my inability to locate one of my sermons which I mention what he did for me...just wanted to send him a copy....so I write this article to tell José García something I've been wanting to tell him for decades. Thank you for saving my life. May this article find you well my brother.

Roca's 'Cock'

"Do not entertain an accusation against an elder unless it is brought by two or three witnesses" (1Tim.5.19)

Orad Sin Cesar Society (Pray Without Ceasing Society) informants were agents of a secret society that would infiltrate prayer groups in order to extract intelligence which were relayed back to religious leaders. These would be sources of great pleasure or anguish to any clergy listening to them. Raja's ecclesiastical investigations were often triggered by these gossip mongers-like agents. One such incident was a growing story going through the religious community that old time conservative Pastor Roca was involved in pornographic activities. This reportedly grew out from observing folks from the neighborhood walking by Roca's while making loud insinuations about betting on the pastor's male privates. Strangely enough, unchurched members of the neighborhood never explicitly accused Roca of sexual inappropriateness. Still, members of sister churches were alarmed about ongoing reports coming from O.S.C. secret agents. Raja bumped into the neighborhood heckler Sinvergüenza. He greeted and treated him to an early morning café con leche y pan tostado con mantequilla. As they engaged in a small chitchat, Raja purposely accompanied him through the neighborhood where Pastor Roca's church was located. When they were walking by the church, Sinvergüenza started in a heckling voice, making a loud comment, but then restrained himself. Raja asked him what the story was behind the rumors of the pastor's sexual indiscretion. He looked puzzled at first and then laughingly began to bring clarity to the situation the O.S.C. 'prayerfully ' anguished over.

Dear Tabla,
Pastor Roca came to the South Bronx a couple of years ago to pastor a small dwindling congregation. He had great old time charisma and his church loved dogmatic stands against modern music, new fashions,

tattoos, owning pitbulls, and so on. His church slowly grew with folks and families new to this country and those blaming their families' failures on an Americanized lenient and tolerant lifestyle. He became the local ultra conservative hero, bashing nearby pastors for 'selling out morally'. Now Pastor Roca did have a leisuretime hobby. He spent time raising a pet rooster. This rooster was no ordinary rooster. The strict clergy had fed this fowl his special blend of natural steroid-like bird feed. The bird grew into a powerful, muscular and ferocious rooster which the pastor would train to attack and rip heavy leather poles. The pastor heard from one of his elders about an illegal cock fighting basement in Queens and all the big bucks that were betted over there. Although he wasn't interested in the money, his pride did make him ponder how great he would feel seeing his specially trained rooster be victorious over the other feathered fighters. One Sunday he arranged for a guest speaker to speak in his place at church. Pastor Roca disguised himself and drove with his pride and joy over to the Queens-based illegal cock fight where nobody knew him. He entered his rooster unto the fight ring. The crowd began betting their hard earned minimum wage money. Pastor Roca was more focused on the anticipation of seeing his little Rocky tear the other rooster apart....until he heard from the crowd....'I want to bet 50 bucks on the Preacher's cock!!!'. Thus, that afternoon Sinvergüenza's shout out from the crowd began circulating as an ongoing community's inside joke with the O.S.C. eventually holding the wrong end of the rooster incident.

Behind The Curtain

"…but we have renounced the things hidden because of shame, not walking in craftiness or adulterating the word of God, but by the manifestation of truth commending ourselves to every man's conscience in the sight of God" (2 Corinthians 4:2)

The three consecutive Ayes (Woes) were announced from the pulpit one evening by Pastor Salamanca. He allegedly had the spiritual gifts of the word of knowledge and discernment. This was a usual late evening weekly prophetic warning with the public notice that the individual being warned by the Holy Spirit was seated in the audience. These specific spiritual gifts, according to certain theologians, is the ability given to a person through the Holy Spirit to suddenly know things as well to be able to read peoples' intentions. The spooky delivered woes (ayes in Spanish which is derived of the Hebrew ove) were modern day versions of the warnings given by prophets to Israel in Old Testament times. These particular ayes would identify specific transgressions, their consequences as well as opportunities to turn away from these sins. That same evening , as if it was a treat, Salamanca gleefully announced that he was sponsoring a world traveling speaker. This special guest was promoted as having a higher level of these same supernatural gifts the pastor often displayed, but with the additional gift of supernatural healing. A member of Pastor Salamanca's church was David. An upset David confided his disappointment in having once met this announced big icon in the POWER, MIRACLES & PROPHETIC AWE supernatural ministries. Back then he excitedly engaged his super hero in a church lobby. During a brief conversation David told him his heart's desires. Later that same evening the celebrated grifter did a word of knowledge act using a shocked and paralyzed David in the audience. David was spectacularly told what his desired goals were in a public manner that would leave spectators thinking that this was supernatural affirming revelation. Raja listened compassionately remembering his own childhood experience with David's own pastor. Raja once injured himself goofing around in school, playing martial arts, and fibbed to his mother attributing his injury to a staircase misstep. Raja's mom called David's pastor for transportation. In the car on the way to the medical clinic, Pastor Salamanca asked Raja how he got hurt and the fib was repeated. When the pastor accepted the story, Raja thought to himself, 'Nah, This guy doesn't have those powers'.

Tato was a kind hearted young man loved by his community. Still, he was the butt of many folks' jokes because of his stuttering. But his stuttering did not stop him from having a beautiful singing voice. Like so many great singers and songwriters such as B.B. King, Carly Simon, and Bill Withers , whom themselves stuttered, Tato turned to music and singing to express himself. It was rumored that one time he had visitors at his home that his parents were entertaining. They instructed Tato that under no circumstances he should interrupt the adults conversations. So the parents and the guests were in the living room enjoying good conversation. Tato kept walking back-and-forth from the kitchen and the bathroom while holding a small glass of water. Finally his parents stopped in and demanded him to explain himself. He anxiously tried to tell them but had an extra difficulty that evening with his stuttering. The parents then told him to sing the reason. Tato then began singing " It's really Bad!! I'm not kidding Dad! I'm really trying to be Calm!! But it's really bad Mom!, All this water I acquire is because kitchen is on fire!! ". The fire was eventually snuffed out and the parents worked on having better communications with their boy. Anyways, now Tato was peer pressured into going to the POWER & MIRACLES revival tent meeting. Raja accompanied Tato and David to the tent one evening. He was hoping to be moral support to Tato and to stop David from making a scene. At the end of the revival service Pastor Raja, Tato and David left elated and laughing.

Dear Tabla- The visiting self-styled POWER & MIRACLES faith healer told the audience to sing loudly to God using one of his patented healing songs while he escorted the lame man with a crutch into back side of the stage's curtain. The audience sang the popular song in a frenzy. The faith healer came out from behind the curtain holding the crutch and announcing 'Se sano!! Alaba!!' (He's healed!!! Praise!!!) And the audience broke out in loud applause. The next person in the healing line was Tato who walked up to the faith healer asking for healing from his terrible stuttering. The healing celebrity escorted Tato behind the curtains, giving the audience the same instructions. The audience loudly sang and swayed as to entice deity for a showtime miracle. The healer again comes out from behind the stage curtains and announces 'Se sano!!! Esta hablando claramente!!! Alaba!! (He's healed!!! He's speaking clearly!! Praise!!!!) The audience broke out in applause, cardio dancing, shouts and cab calling whistles. Suddenly a loud crash sound came from behind the stage. The worshipped healer turned around and yelled 'What was that?!!!'. High beautiful singing voice from behind the curtain 'Se callo el cojo!!' (The lame guy fell down).

You Don't Remember Me But...

Be not forgetful to entertain strangers: for thereby some have entertained angels unawares. Hebrews 12:3

Raja arrived with Tesoro home one late weekend evening after a morning men's prayer service quite pensive and humbled. The week before he was feeling aggravated with a new church member that was crossing boundaries. Raja had started pastoral counseling with one of the members of his congregation. This member had been struggling with anger issues. The new member, an older gentleman, began making moves to take the struggling member under his wings for mentoring addressing the issues at hand. It turns out that the new member, Dr. Agradecido, had a anger management counseling business. Raja expressed to his wife Tesoro that he felt that the new member was out of line. It wasn't unusual for new charismatic members have ulterior motives to take new members under their wings in order to start a new church. Pied piper personalities sneakingly harvesting from where they did not plant with hardships. At church leadership conventions highly paid church growth motivational speakers would display geographic charts showing supposedly impressive explosion of new churches as a result of their patented strategies. Raja often would recognize that a portion of these new churches were the result of church divisions and not necessarily resulting from new souls from the area. Tesoro gently told Raja that he may have to put his own pastoral ego in check and directly meet with his new member to probe his intentions as well as set boundaries. Later that week Raja confronted the man at a men's prayer service. The man apologized for not being acquainted with church's protocol and told Raja "Pastor, let me assure you that I didn't come to plant discord. I came in indebtedness. You don't remember me do you? Well, I remember you". After the men's prayer service Raja arrived home, kissed Tesoro, entered his prayer area for introspection of his own heart and to journal.

Dear Tabla,

Today I became defensive with a brother that only meant to gratefully be a blessing to me, my family and church family. After he clarified his intentions with a startling backstory, I apologized. He was gracious with a thank you that now made sense. I had actually met Dr. Agradecido ages ago. So I found the moment in an old Jesus Freak journal of mine. So while still holding the gun he showed us he asked me of what did God heal me.... It started when I decided to go down to Harlem 125th St. to give out those annoying gospel tracts. I was 17. There were two gentlemen from a Spanish Pentecostal church that were also distributing tracts on the same street. They looked at my long hair, goatee and carpenter pants. After a short talk with them they invited me to give out gospel tracts along with them.... Excuse my rambling, it really started when I was under a lot of physical pain. You see from age 14 to about age 17, I had been conditioning my body with rigid exercising and also preparing for martial arts training. After I decided to surrender my life to Christ Jesus as Lord my lower back began giving me serious problems. I lost my flexibility and I was in constant pain. I was prescribed strong pain medication that I reluctantly and sparingly took. I would ask God to relieve me from this pain, but the pain continued -at times it got worse. That did not stop me from believing in His word and trusting Him. One time out of frustration I decided to go to into Harlem and give out gospel tracts. As we were giving out these a gentleman walked by us who was stopped by the two brothers that has invited me to join them. Apparently he was a former member of their church. According to them he had been healed sometime ago of very serious condition. Healing was not something I was in the mood to hear about. They asked him how he was doing and why he had not been in fellowship with them. He then began to tell them about how bad his marriage was in that at that moment he was on his way to kill his wife and her secret lover. He did this while pulling out a gun and showing us the weapon he intended to use. They each try to persuade him that he should not do that and that he should trust the God that had healed him. They each told him about their own personal encounter with God's mighty healing and how grateful they were. He listened to them with a respectful indifference and then looked at me and asked me for my healing story. I began to tell him how everything physically went wrong for me at the time I decided to let God be the manager of my life. I told him about the great physical pain I was enduring, show him how I had great difficulty even walking. Then I explained that I had surrendered my life to a loving God -whether He meets my needs here on earth or not, he was worthy to be surrendered to. I guess my story stunned him, it was not what he expected to hear but it came from my heart. He, now known to me as Dr. Agradecido, gave his gun to the two gentlemen who escorted him to their church building. I was too much pain to follow them and went back home. It was a painfully good day.

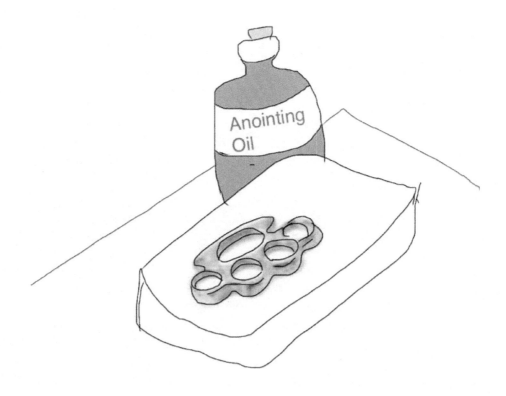

Gangster Grandma

"Whatever your hand finds to do, do it with all your might,…" (Ecclesiastes 9:10)

Church missionaries were the backbone of many small churches. These weren't vacationing males traveling to exotic lands and coming back with tales of thousands of souls getting saved in return for a hefty love offering. These were usually strong females full of nitty gritty love for their communities and always gave Christ the credit. Sister Misericordia was one of these. She always found ways to help needy families who often in curious gratitude would drop by the church to attend a few services. Some of them would move on and some would of them would eventual stay as church members. Recently Misericordia has been helping folks in the community as well as those in the church experiencing issues of domestic violence. Encouraging them and helping them navigate systems in order to get them to safe places. She reminded Raja of his own belated grandmother.

Dear Tabla,

One 1968 summer day my grandmother church missionary Hermana Ramona Guerrera de Dios took notice that one of her converts Inocencia had not been attending church for a period of a week. I accompanied my abuela (grandma) to the supermarket to pick up some groceries. After shopping we took a short walk over to Inocencia's home. Abuela knocked on the door and Inocencia answered. Abuela looked at her and inquired "What happened?". There stood Inocencia, single parent of five children, sporting a huge black and blue eye. She let us in and she told us an astounding story while she served us coffee and crackers. Apparently she was being bullied by the building superintendent's wife who for some reason took a huge dislike to Inocencia. She had physically attacked Inocencia and left her with bruises. Inocencia did not report it to the police and had been staying home fearfully avoiding another unprovoked attack. Then I saw it in grandma's eyes. It was there in almost incarnate form…. The life living manifestation of her last name… guerrera de Dios…. Warrior of God. She gently whispered assurances into Inocencia's ears and then laid her prayer warrior hands over her. In her intercessory prayer she quoted an old testament phrase "Amos 5:24: "But let justice roll down like waters, and righteousness like an everflowing stream."

That summer evening after church my grandmother took upon herself to bring a group of church numbers to a building where a bruised up sister from our church lived and was being bullied by the super's wife. On the way there I recognized the building in my hands got cold and clammy. On the stoops in front of the entrance there was a rough tough crowd listening to music, cursing and drinking beer. Abuela and I walked toward Inocencia first floor apartment while the rest of the church members spoke and tried to evangelize the rowdy group. When Inocencia answered the door grandma inquired who the bully lady was and she pointed out a tall big boned woman standing with the thuggish group. Abuela approached the lady and asked if she could speak with her for a moment away from the group. The Godzilla body type woman followed grandma halfway through the lobby and listened to abuela. She looked at abuela's huge Bible and began to tell her in a mocking manner that she had no use for religion. Then I saw the carnage coming. Inocencia was sneaking behind the lady and all of a sudden she sucker punched the giant in the back of the head with a rabbit punch. Then followed up with a couple of kidney blows. The stunned woman turned around to see a powerful feather weight boxing Inocencia. Immediately Abuela dropped her Bible and held the woman in a full behind the neck Nelson hold while Inocencia followed up with a flurry of body shots. Abuela then yelled "ENOUGH" released the lady and quickly intercepted Inocencia's throat punch set up. The lady then began yelling and screaming that this was a set up. Till this day I don't quite know how we were able to leave that area alive and without one hair on our bodies damaged. All I know is that from there that day on that Goliath of a woman did not bother Inocencia again. She now happily enjoyed strutting her way over to church without fear.

The Fela & Franco Mess

"See to it that no one falls short of the grace of God and that no bitter root grows up to cause trouble and defile many" (Hebrews 12:15)

Two well liked and highly regarded elders were dear Sister Fela and dear Brother Franco. Fela was known for her passion of learning and reciting beautiful poetry and long passages of scriptures. She had the gift of hospitality welcoming many of the youth who were friends of her children to come to her home where she would cook delicious and abundant meals for them. Franco was very popular with children, loaning them simple handheld musical instruments in church for them to worship during services. He also carried pockets full of wrapped candy to give to the kids after church services. Now for a few weeks Fela seemed very bothered by Franco's presence. It was rumored that the sister may have learned of something sinister regarding Franco and his attraction to children. Their pastor , Rev. Paco, was very concerned about this situation and had asked Raja for assistance. There was an all night prayer watch service happening at Fela's and Franco's Church one Friday evening and Raja was invited as a special guest. It was customary for church members to ask for or were delegated to take 'a part' during a prayer break during these long prayer gatherings. This meant that the members would have access to the front of the sanctuary and either speak to the congregation, sing, testify, preach or even confess a transgression. This often happened during breaks in all night (through next morning) prayer services. That late 'vigilia' evening Raja pulled Sister Fela and Brother Franco before they took any part in speaking from the front of the sanctuary. Their hearts had to be right, transparent and free from any foul thoughts before attempting any spiritual edifying communication from the front of the sanctuary.

Dear Tabla,

Today Rev. Paco asked me to attend their evening vigilia so I could observed Fela and Franco closely. There seemed to be a lot of tension between the two elders. I took aside Franco and inquired what was the source of tension between them two. He told me he did not know where the hostility toward him from Sister Fela was coming from. Franco verbalized feeling very sad and apprehensive whenever she was nearby. A moment later I spoke with Sister Fela in private to which she admitted having anger toward the brother but did not feel comfortable disclosing it to me. I then ask her if I could pray over her and she gave me permission to lay hands on her forehead. I prayed that the Lord would pour the freedom into the heart to open up to leadership regarding her anger or apprehension toward brother Franco. That there will be no disharmony among the fellowship as well as there being a safe place through Christ's presence whenever two or three are gathered in His name. Later on Sister Fela took a public speaking part during the vigilia. She asked for prayer and confessed a deep resent against fellow church member Franco. She told us that she been faithfully keeping the church clean on a volunteer basis during the week at a great exhausting sacrifice. But that she had been holding a grudge against Hermano Franco because whenever he uses the men's restroom he doesnt flush and he leaves long thick 'mojones' (Spanish slang for feces). Well, I'm just grateful that we were able to clean up that mess of a discord.

Sermon Friendly Fires

But Jesus answered, "No more of this!" (Luke 22:51)

A church reached out to Raja to be their special motivational speaker. The dynamic speaker they had contracted for that night pulled out at the last minute and they needed a last minute substitute . They wanted replacement invited guest Pastor Rajatabla to inspire the congregation to be bold about their faith. So Raja delivered the good deed, passionately preaching his heart out. A week after Raja covered for the preferred preacher, the church complained to the denomination's headquarters that he had spoken very harshly using profanity . Missionary Snow heard about the situation and contacted Raja. Raja had used the terms ' Ñoña and Ñoñados' . Which turned out , unbeknownst to Raja, to be vulgar terms to listeners at the church he had preached at. The missionary advocated for Raja at the governing body's offices assuring them that no malice was intended.

Dear Tabla,

A couple days ago I was angry at the ungratefulness of the pastor and his church which had asked me to help them out at short notice. Later they accused me of being very vulgar from their pulpit. Apparently the insincere pastor and his congregation did not really want to be encouraged and exhorted to live a more effective godly life for Christ. An old professor and missionary Brother Snow heard about the situation and met with the pastor and his church members. It turns out that in the household I was raised in the Spanish terms, 'Ñoña and Ñoñados' were used in the less vulgar manner. At home it meant a person that was spoiled and softened or the act of spoiling and softening a person to be virtually useless. But outside my household in many other Spanish speaking households and countries the term referred to soft feces or becoming a pile of excrement. Pretty gross when you think about it. Anyways, this was explained to me and the misunderstanding explained to the pastor in church. Thanks to Brother Snow's intervention there was much happy reconciliation. As I thanked my dear retired professor, he also thanked me for a past misunderstanding and intervention.

When I was a Bible school student and intern at a church, Missionary Professor Snow and his wife gave a presentation of their work in South America. So as they gave a slideshow presentation at one point there was a picture of Sister Snow holding a South American critter by the tail. She then announced through the speaker in Spanish "here I am holding a critter". Unfortunately the term for critter she used was "bichos". Now that term for her in South America and would mean critter but for the Spanish speaking audience she was doing the presentation for it was a vulgar term for penis. So there I was shocked but understanding what the misunderstanding would be and hoped that the audience understood. So while I looked at the congregants as they were looking at each other wide-eyed there was another slide that popped up. It was Brother Snow holding up two critters. I scrambled for a piece of paper and a pen to pass a note to Sister Snow but it did not make it to her before she made the next announcement. "There is my husband brother snow holding two bichos!!!" I finally got the note to her with the hopes that they were no other slides with an orgy of critters. They weren't such pictures and she continued the presentation calmly and without missing a beat. The term bicho stopped making appearances that night.

As I thanked Brother Snow, we continued to reminisce about our time at the Bible College where I was a student and he a professor. We laughed over one memory. It was a Bible College where all students and faculty members were required to attend early morning chapel services prior to the school day's classes. The meeting consisted of corperate praying, singing, worshiping and listening to a faculty member or visiting clergy deliver a sermon or word of inspiration. Brother Cornerstone, in his late eighties, was loved by all. He was a legend in our movement. Although sometimes he would stumble across words, pause for clarity of thought, we all would respectfully wait...and he never disappointed us. It was his turn to speak this morning. He was telling us about the night Jesus was betrayed, how Saint Peter took a sword and cut a Roman soldier's ear off. We were all tired and anxious over mid-terms. Brother Cornerstone suddenly misspoke when he got to the climax of the story when the soldier approached Jesus: "and then one of the disciples took out a concealed sword, swung it with all his might, and cut the soldier's peter off!!!". First we were awakened and startled...then we all bursted out laughing nearly peeing on ourselves ....Brother Cornerstone lost his preaching composure in laughter. We were dismissed early that day and feeling less stressed about midterm exams.

She Lies!!! She Lies!!!

"Sin will drag you deeper than the grave"
(Pastor Raja)

Church Deacon Trustee Esteban took upon himself to be the keeper of the Senda Antigua (ancient path). He prided himself to be a purist and keeper of authentic Christianity. He often debated with the pastor over the church needing a stricter code of 'Disciplina' (discipline), more than implying that Raja was ruining the ministry with a weak permissive gospel. Under this dogmatic code a church member being disciplined would not be allowed to participate in much cherished spotlighted type of church activities. Such activities include singing solos, speaking to the congregation from the front of the sanctuary, leading special projects, etc. They were however graciously not banned from contributing financially to the church. Disciplina usually fell heavier on the female congregants than on the male congregants. In some churches male offenses worthy of disciplina included wearing colored shirts, cologne, perfumes and jewelry. Long list of ladies' transgressions included hair trimming, eye brow plucking, leg shaving, makeup, wearing anything resembled pants, and pierced earrings. Esteban always took an opportunity in church trustee meetings to insinuate that Raja was too much of a candy coating preacher being soft on sin. One Sunday Raja preached on the topic of what sin was and what it was not. While also coming to the point of the seriousness of this subject, he used one of his favorite illustration of a cocky young man named Pitó and his pet python Pecado. Pitó lived in a rough neighborhood where pitbull fighting was a popular street sport. He purchased a small pet neck snake which she nurtured lovingly. One day he came to a pit dog fight with a duffel bag. Pitó unzipped the duffel bag, whistled and a small snake head started coming out and the crowd laughed. Someone in the crowd yelled out look he bought some dog food!!! The crowd's laughter slowly decreased as they saw the snake slither slowly out of the bag increasingly revealing a massive body. As the python wrestled with its large pitbull competitor it manage to strategically immobilize the dog's hind legs and then able to squeeze the life out of it. Pitó and his pet python Pecado became very popular. One day and trying to impress some young ladies, Pitó whistled and had Pecado wrap him up completely. As the girls in the neighborhood cheerred, applaud and whistled in admiration they heard screams and crunching sounds coming from within the massive snake. Animal control arrived and managed to get the reptile to uncoil. Pitó was found lifeless. The servant had subtlety become the master and the master had 'trágicamente' become the slave. And that is how it is with sin. It slowly kills you and will cunningly drag you deeper than the grave. At the end of the sermon there was an outburst from the congregation , thus revealing sin in the camp.

Dear Tabla- A year ago today Church Deacon Trustee Esteban was asleep during the my sermon. One woman was tearfully moved by the message on sin and went up to the altar for prayer when I finished delivering my sermon. Since we were closing the service, I called out for Deacon Esteban to lead the congregation in a closing prayer. One of the church members nudged Esteban. He awoke only to see the shapely woman up front of the church crying uncontrollably and the congregation staring at him. Esteban jumped up from the bench yelling 'Ella Miente!! Ella Miente!!' (She Lies!! She Lies!!). Some in the congregation rationalized that he was protesting the woman's tight clothing. Most weren't so naïve. Esteban didn't stay around to explain himself nor submit himself to church leadership and pastoral leadership. It was reported through the grapevine that the deacon established a church with strict dogmatic dress codes which he pastored for a short time. Apparently there was a police unit called to his church to save Esteban from a young man that had him in a wicked choke hold. Reportedly there was a young female member that was being physically seduced by the former deacon when the jealous boy friend came into their church building. Esteban has moved on to start his own religious denomination. The young lady and young man currently are happily serving in our small church's usher and security ministries.

Mavi and The Scriptures

"Keep this Book of the Law always on your lips; meditate on it day and night, so that you may be careful to do everything written in it. Then you will be prosperous and successful"
(Joshua 1:8)

Raja spent a night in the church fervently praying often staring at the attendance offering wall wooden plaque. At times that wall item appeared to be a taunting score card for visiting clergy to see. Other times it was a thorn in Raja's side trying to teach church members to help keep the little church's financial health sustainable. Raja's had a constant disagreement with the church elders and trustees about the purpose of Pro Templo (church building fund raising) activities. This specific type of fundraising was not for paying for maintenance or rent. But they would just stubbornly move on with their fund raising activities. Raja just shook his head, remembering that even Jesus' own disciples wanted to teach Him about leadership. Now there was Pro Templo pasteles fierce food competition with volunteer cooks arguing over which one had the best recipes. Sister Ramona organized a tambourine percussions competition charging members of other churches a fee for entering. It was customary at the small store front church to invite visitors of the Faith to come to the front to say, recite or sing something. It was a cold winter without a tree leaf to be found in the South Bronx, when a visitor whistled a Pentecostal ballad in the church. Folks were immensely blessed that evening. The next week an inspired church brother Bobby wanted to demonstrate his percussion skills by using a cupped hand under his armpit. The brother then organized a whistling and armpit music concert in an effort to help raise funds for the church. Sister Maria, who constantly asked Raja for scriptural references regarding dogmatic matters, was in a sharp polemic dispute with Brother Velez for his making and selling Mavi.It is a Taino word. Mavi is a fermented drink made from the bark of the mavi tree which is also known as mabetree, soldierwood, or seaside buckthorn and can be found from Southern Florida all the way to Guatemala. This refreshing drink is somewhat like a root beer and there supposedly are no other drinks similar to it. Sister Maria came from another subculture within Hispanic Pentecostalism that associated Mavi with all other forbidden alcoholic beverages. Some of the congregants had nicked named her behind her back- Sister Anti- Mavi Maria. All this fuss and activity, but few members wanted to address that the church would most likely lose its lease due to finances. Many members were sending money to bigger and better branded sparkly ministries. Kinda like in the movie There Will Be Blood, the bigger religious businesses were drinking our milk shake.

Dear Tabla,
What a roller coaster day today was. I've been trying to lead my congregation into sound planning. I was so afraid of losing our church space by not being able to pay the rent on our leased location. Church members not quite registering that typical faithful offerings and tithing would not necessarily be burdensome to them and would keep our church location open. Many of them seemed just to be enamored of remembering their childhood in a small cozy church but not understanding of the importance of payments for things as such utilities. For years they have been doing emergency fundraising activities to make rent payments that could've been covered by simple consistent offerings and tithing. It's not like they have a full salaried pastor on board. The monthly stipend I receive is sufficient for me to buy an inexpensive fast food breakfast. The revenue that was generated through the recent fundraising events has turned out to be enough to pay a portion of the upcoming rent and utilities. I went downtown to walk through some of the scenic parts of our city, enjoying one of our large parks. After a while I walked out of the park

still meditating and pensive about our church financial situation and whether I should continue pastoring. As I waited for the street light to cross the street, I stood near a homeless man that was laying down on the pavement. All of a sudden he sat up and began singing "What do you think about my Jesus!" he kept singing this part of a song which I knew from my childhood. He sang it to all the people walking by who ignored him. I thought that I would surprise him by singing the response to that song once he would sing it toward me. So the brief moment came where he looked at me and saying "What do you think about my Jesus?". With a big smile on my face I sang the response "He's all right, he's all right!!". Then the man looked at me square in the eye and saying "So why are you worrying about money?". With that he stood up took his belongings and walked away from me without asking for any money. I took that moment as some sort of disguised angel message from God and made my way back home. As I arrived to my lower income part of the city I walked by the church. There was Sister Anti-Mavi Maria waiting for someone to open up the church. I asked her why she was waiting and if she had an appointment. She bowed her head and handed me an envelope which to my surprise had a huge amount of money. It turns out that she been secretly playing the lotto on a regular basis (A big taboo in the majority of our churches) and in her last few ticket purchases she had been using the numeric scripture references she asked from me in order to play. And she hit the lotto big time. She asked me to inform the church leadership and members that I received this money from an anonymous donor. I told her that I would under other circumstances refuse to take the money based on some straight laced spirituality but I rebuke that ungrateful spirit. Mavi Maria's posture loosened up and said "Well then, I'll drink to that".

Musical Tantrums & Ransoms

"Don't hang out with angry people; don't keep company with hotheads. Bad temper is contagious— don't get infected." (Proverbs 22:24)

Bishop Mack was frantic as he contacted Raja. His church was broken into and most of the musical instruments and electronic music systems were stolen. There was a world renowned media company that had selected his church to produce a documentary about urban churches and their musical talents. The Bishop's church was selected out of hundreds in the city for this documentary. Bishop Mack was known to be a very big hearted pastor to which many outcast former members of other churches gravitated to. The bishop had the knack of identifying talents and skills and put them to use at his church. Many talents and gifts bloomed and blossomed beautifully under his nurturing. As his congregation grew its popularity also grew. The bishop's inclinations to gather many disgruntled members started to lack wisdom in screening them when it came to granting them significant roles in his church service ministries.

Dear Tabla,
After meeting with the bishop today, and consoling him regarding the theft of equipment, I returned to our church to let in a couple of volunteers who help with the maintenance of our own sanctuary. I was greeted by Ishmael AKA Bugsy who recently started attending our church and expressed wanting to become a member. He had a load of musical equipment and inquired where could he store them in the church. I invited him in to my office area for a little talk. It turned out that Bugsy was a talented musician and wanted to bless our church with his gifts. He owned the best of musical equipments and wanted them situated in the sanctuary where he could lead the church's music ministry. When I asked

if he heard about the break in robbery that occurred at Bishop Mack's church, Bugsy broke out in laughter. It turned out that the missing instruments of the bishop's church were actually Bugsy's property which he abruptly took back without fair warning. After a brief talk it was evident that Bugsy was an ill tempered believer who often used his musical contributions as spiteful leverage. He often jumped from church to church whenever he did not get his way or felt slighted. Bugsy wore his easy to be offended tendencies as though it was a relished badge of honor and enjoyed disrespectfully refusing offered gestures of reconciliation. As he continued to ask me where he could store his instruments I informed him that we would not be able to afford him. He then graciously explained that he would minister in our church for free. I asked Bugsy if he would consider meeting with Bishop Mack and work toward a civil fence-mending. He laughed and thought I was joking. Bugsy appeared to be under the impression that I would not want to miss out on having him, his invaluable talents and his instruments ministering at our church. I respectfully explained to him that I and the church would not have the seasoned capacity to pay the price of having someone who practices anger participating in ministering to the congregation. It wasn't Pentecost tongues of fire that I saw on Bugsy's head but rather fumes as he left my company in a huff. As he reloaded his equipment into his van he turned around and glared at me. Lord forgive me, I could not help myself and commented towards him, "And anyways we are greatly blessed with cutting edge wind armpits and whistling musicians"

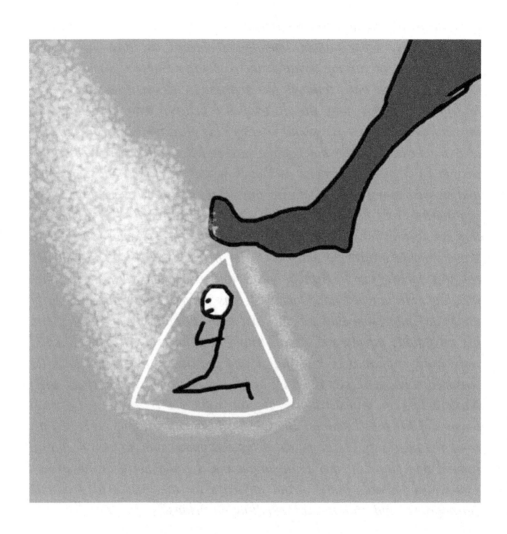

Workplace Persecutions

"God is to us a God of deliverances…"
(Psalm 68:20)

At his secular job, Raja was being given a hard time by clinicians due to him being a Pentecostal. The job site bullies entertained themselves doing half baked jobs and sabotaging Raja's assignments. They told him to administration that Raja was preoccupied trying to proselytize patients and discriminating against ones whose lifestyles contrast against his belief system. In actuality they became defensive and worried that he would not goof off during work time nor short change residence of the community. Many workers held a strong disdain toward the community which mirrored the poor services they rendered. Raja's discontent with coworkers poor work festered to rage when discrimination played out in referrals being misplaced and discarded. He decides to not surrender to his enragement and prayerfully stay calm as a dove and lucid a serpent in a den of wolves. Holy Spirit cunning led him to prayer. Raja was of the opinion that prayer shouldn't be escapism but rather vigilance. One day he was asked to help with a glitch with the main computer that was messing up the functions of all the other devices. The IT department was taking a long time and an aggravated admin pulled Raja in to troubleshoot due to his having a Midas touch with computer stuff. Something told Raja to suppress his "not my job" union member self and help out even at the cost of being accused by fellow workers of brown nosing. So there he was going through long lines of data and suddenly like a vision of divine clarity THERE IT WAS.... In soft ecstatic whispered volume, Raja praised the Lord in tongues, which spooked two of his persecuting coworkers, Freída and Amber, who where walking by. The computer problem was solved while two workers walked into the administrator's office to complain. Moments later Raja was called into the Lions Den.

Dear Tabla,

Today my administrator who appeared to have a very aggravating week called me into his office. When I came in I saw two of my coworkers sitting down by his desk. I was invited to come closer and sit down. The administrator opened the conversation by thanking me for helping with the computer networks meltdown and then wanted to address some concerns regarding my work ethic. She commended me for the fine performance in caring for the clients assigned to me, but was concerned regarding allegations that my religious views may be tainting the needs of the clients. She asked my colleagues to share their observations regarding the allegations against me. Freída began by asking me if it was true that I was an ordained minister. When I affirmed what she and all the rest of the staff already knew, Freída began to insinuate that my vocation as a clergy and vocation as a mental health clinician had conflicting interests which resulted in biased based disservice to our mental health patients in need. I turned to the administrator and inquired if there were any such complaints that came directly from any current or past patients. She then responded that there were no such complaints, but just concerns recently arisen by coworkers, particularly the two in the office. Earlier I had prayed to God to please clarify persecution, clarify confrontation and clarify courage in my life. I pulled out a floppy disk from my guayabera's extra large pocket and held it up for all to see. I proceeded to present the fact that my caseload was larger than anyone working on the floor and all reports were completed and finalized in a timely fashion. This was due to my doing work from home, and that would be the unethical behavior as a family member and union member that I would intend to cease doing from now on. Then looking at Freída I inquire about her accent which she identified as South African. Then I relayed that I had found that all of the African-American patients who were pregnant and assigned to her were given follow up appointments for abortions and tube tying (tubal ligation) procedures. I continued to ask her if accusing her, an caucasian South Africa of using her position to conduct genocide would be as slanderous as her accusing me of being unethical to my patients because of my religious stance on abortion. Amber's eyes widen as she looked at Freida in disgust . Then I told him that I also saw a discrepancy with the cases and referrals that were sent to Amber. It seems that all the cases with a particular range of birthdates were either deleted or deflected to other colleagues. It was no secret that Amber was a horoscope fanatic. Could it be that she was discarding cases that were not compatible to her own astrological sign. Amber began to protest that astrology was a proven science, but then stopped short of denying that she was discriminating against patients because of their stars. The administrator apologetically thanked me and dismissed me from her office and my two agitators remained. Rumors are that they were escorted from the clinic by security leaving behind their ID badges. Other rumors were that they broke out in a fight in the administrators office resulting in their being dismissed. Other rumors were that God busted a move and that I rocked. I would like to think that the Lord anointed me to be favored by top dragons.

Love You But Don't Gotta Trust You

"But Jesus knew what was in their hearts, and he would not let them have power over him" (John 2:24)

Raja and Tesoro travelled across town to pick up some items they saw on sale. They had a low maintenance lifestyles and we're not bondservants to brand names. Tesoro tapped Raja's shoulder and pointed to a building where several police cars were parked at a couple of years ago. The building had belonged to a well known religious organization with a historical reputation for social justice. Raja had worked there part time as a counselor. The organization liked his demeanor and (especially) that he was a credentialed minister. Although not credentialed with them, they apparently liked the idea of having both a trained counselor and unofficial chaplain for the price of one. A couple of months into his employment their staff were very unpleased with how rudely he had treated a prestigious client. This resulted in Raja being let go. Raja had enjoyed working there before this incident. His only felt aggravation while working there, was an inconvenient glitch with the payroll. He had to go all the way downtown to pick up his paycheck at the organization's divisional headquarters, while the local staff enjoyed the convenience of getting their biweekly salary in cash at the site. Tesoro interlocked her arm with her husband as they continued walking away from the building and remembering God's covering over them in the midst of disappointments.

Dear Tabla,
Had a lovely afternoon with my sweetheart Tesoro shopping for some sales and discounts. We walked by one of my old job sites where I had been employed for a very short time. It was a very good religious organization that helped many needy families and advocated for them. Juanita from the neighborhood came to the head of that ministry, Major

Solberg , asking for help. Her son Peter had been arrested and going to court at a nearby state with the charges of drug trafficking. The Major knew Peter ever since he was a youngster in the neighborhood. With the support and influence of that ministry the young man had greatly thrived educationally to the level that he became an adjunct professor at a very prestigious Ivy League University. Now he had been arrested and appeared to most likely get a severe sentence. The court judge took note of Major's presence during the proceedings and allowed him to advocate for Peter. The judge had great respect for the historic organization that Mayor Solberg represented and gave him custody of Peter as long as he attended mandated counseling. The Major assigned Peter's mandated counseling to me and asked me to figure out what made him tick. It was a well dressed and manicured Peter I met at the small office allotted to me. I we sat down he asked for my credentials and wanted me to explain to him how I was qualified to counsel him, a highly accomplished educated man. Shifting from my innate sense of heated indignation over to trusting God's refining fire, I lovingly pointed out that I wasn't there to be screened by him rather he was there because he grandly messed up. We had a very sobering talk slowly entering a path of what I thought would be mutual respect. As we ended the session I needed to step out and I asked Peter to please step out the office while I lock it up. After a couple of sessions Peter asked me why did he needed to step out and why I locked off the office as well as not allow him to enter the office at the times he came to appointments early or before the office was open. I then pointedly informed him that although I loved him, I wasn't necessarily mandated to trust him. The staff took wind of my brief hallway conversation with Peter and confronted me saying that I needed to be more understanding and compassionate. I stood my ground, and resentment from the staff brewed. They would mockingly refer to me as Reverendo Reventado (equivalent to Reverend Busted Gasket) .Shortly after the Major informed me that he would not be able to keep me on board for budget reasons. He however gave me a few paid days off. The day before I took those freebie days I met with Peter for our last session together. He looked contrite that day and disclosed that he had been struggling with his deep love of scheming and plotting. There appeared to be a breakthrough. As we departed from the office area he overheard staff wishing me farewell from working there. Peter then looked at me and asked if I was really leaving, when I responded that it was true, he smiled telling me that he was sorry to hear that. After a few days off I returned to get some of my office knickknacks and greeted some of the somber looking staff. I was informed that Peter had been volunteering at the site. The custodian Justino had the duty of picking up the biweekly cashed payroll from the bank. He took a liking to Peter who he let assist him in order to build up his morale. After picking up the cash payroll Justino went into a bodega to pick some café, leaving Peter in the ministry's spanking new van to avoid any parking tickets. When Justino returned with the coffee....no van...no payroll...no Peter. But I was still able to pickup my pay from the downtown headquarters. What was meant for my aggravation, God meant it for a Whoah Holy Cow moment for me.

Rivers of Living Waters

"When pride comes, then comes disgrace, but with the humble is wisdom" (1 Peter 5:5)

Well known Evangelist Goya disliked any form of honoring female pastors. This particular evangelist also sought to persuade religious organizations to pressure and expel churches with female clergy. Pastor Raja however owed a lot spiritually to women in leadership. Once during a large ministers convention, while invited guest speaker Goya was making anti female clergy innuendos, Raja stormed out the auditorium while yelling, "Goya, You're Full of It!!". Raja was shortly after reprimanded by his denomination's leadership and his credentials suspended for a year. Although Raja respectfully submitted to their authority, he never stopped believing that God doesn't like ugly. A couple of years later the evangelist was again invited to be the main speaker at the annual convention. Goya appeared slimmer and healthier. He requested from the leadership that it'd be Raja who would introduce him to the audience. Although feeling humiliated Raja takes the microphone and gloomily introduced Goya.

Dear Tabla-
Years of a westernized prosperity theological diet of eating red meats, high sodium products, carbs, gluten rich, sugary and carbonated products struck down a celebrated preacher. Evangelist Goya's lower abdomen became very swollen and he hadnt been able to have a bowel movement for weeks. There was nothing medical specialists could do, other than recommend a serious operation. Goya refused the surgical procedure and rather go back to his small home town and pass away peacefully. Upon arrival his family insisted that he visit Pastora Lola for divine healing. Lola was the pastor of a small congregation that met in a small makeshift

church building in a rural part in Puerto Rico. Although Goya always preached against female pastors, he swallowed his pride and travelled to see her. Lola prayed over him and afterwards told Goya that he must forsake eating junk foods, fatty red meats and instead eat vegetables and drink fresh juices...and go use her special Rio de Jordan outhouse by the river seven times. Although years of big city toilet use had made Goya never ever want to return to use wooden latrines of his childhood, he complied with Lola's inspired directions. Day one nothing. Day two nothing. Day three nothing. Day four nothing. Day five nothing. Day six nothing. A year later back in New York after swallowing my pride I introduced Goya at our annual ministerial convention. The main speaker walked uprightly toward the front, took the microphone and began speaking: "Brothers and sisters...I come to you very humbled...after years of mistreating the body God gave me by living a life of gluttony...my bowels refused to work...the mountains of decaying foods inside me began to release deadly toxins throughout my body...butcher-minded doctors just wanted to mutilate my insides...then the Lord brought me back to my roots in Puerto Rico...through Pastora Lola He made me swallow my pride and sit in an uncomfortable outhouse ...day uno nada...day dos nada...day tres nada...day cuatro nada....day cinco nada...day seis nada...but on the seventh day- GLORY TO GOD!!! THAT WAS LIKE RIVERS OF LIVING WATERS!!!" From that night Goya determined to humbly share that testimony at everyplace he had demeaned women in ministry. There have been reports of many male attendees being delivered from constipation of all sorts everywhere Goya shared his broken bondage and lighter load.

The Great Hugging & Chest Bumping Revival

"He is before all things, and in him all things hold together"
(Colossians 1:17)

There was a great revival movement that had mysteriously disappeared as quickly as it had appeared. Folks spoke highly of it and many were disappointed that they did not have the opportunity to attend one of the much acclaimed The Great Hugging and Chest Bumping Revival meetings. Believers from all over the country and the world came to attend one of the meetings only leaving disappointed. Some of the distinct characteristics of the revival included hopping up and down, folks bumping each other chest to chest, yelling in a repentance/remorseful fashion "I accept that no!!" and "Thus Saith The Lord I TOLD YOU NOT TO !!". Raja had been approached by several believers asking him if he could spiritually and forensically find out whatever happened to the revival. Was God unhappy with His people? So Raja went on looking through some of the posted social media pictures of this great revival and he noticed one elusive person that he knew and admired very much. So along with The Hound of Heaven our Pentecostal Private-eye followed the scent.

Dear Tabla,

Today I went on a revival tracking mission. The Great Hugging and Chest Bumping Revival had mysteriously vanished and folks that wanted their blessing were bewildered. Looking through social media pictures of the event I noticed that Pastor Samson had been on the church speaking platform at the time the revival broke out. It was a blurry picture but it was definitely him. He was a huge man of God known not only for his gigantic physique but also even more for his enormous tender heart. The semi retired pastor would go to a nitty-gritty gym to work out early mornings. It was a gym that specialized in old school strength training with none of the fancy modern day exercise equipment. I decided to drop by this morning to greet this slayer of modern day athletes. When I came in there he was leading a small Bible study before his new athletic fans began strength training under him in the ways of old dinosaurs. When Pastor Sampson saw me he excused himself after a short prayer with his group and came over to greet me. Despite his old age the man could still give powerful bearhugs while miraculously not cracking folks ribs. Samson agreed to let me treat him to brunch at a nearby healthy food diner after his training session with his next generation old school exercise people. At the diner I asked Pastor Samson about the revival movement and his place in it. He bowed his head, sighed and then looked at me confiding the behind the scene saga. Samson was invited by Pastor Michelangelo to a revival meeting at his church where Revivalist Gary would be ministering at. Now the revivalist was a very charismatic personality, quite a bit of a showman and very persuasive when asking for financial support for his ministry. Pastor Michelangelo had been working hard leading a church building fundraising campaign and knew that his congregants were already financially stressed out. He had set aside a generous amount of money to bless Gary at the end of the service. At the evening of the revival meeting Pastor Michelangelo and Revivalist Gary were sitting up at the platform in a similar fashion that many churches of the movement would have leadership sit as if they were demigods, overviewing the worship behavior of their audience. Pastor Samson was invited to come to the platform and sit with them as well as witnessed a briefing given to Gary by Michael Angelo. It was explained that there was an offering set aside especially for Gary and it was requested that he would not ask for any special offerings from the already financially stressed out congregants and visitors. After a quite impressive presentation that left the audience in a spiritual frenzy, revivalist took a moment and asked for a special offering for his own ministry. He directed the ushers to move around the audience with baskets. He turned around to give the microphone over and shake the hand of the hosting pastor Michelangelo, who walked over to him with jaw clinched and tight fisted......I TOLD YOU NOT TO.... And he swung at Gary and Gary swung back. Now at the speed that only the Holy Spirit could move, Pastor Sampson immobilized both men together in a bear hug. When the audience saw all three men of God on the platform hugging each other and moving uncontrollably they misinterpreted it as them joyfully hugging and praising God under Holy Ghost power. And that is how the short lived The Great Hugging and Chest Bumping Revival started. Sometimes I wonder if God just amusingly sends me cases like this to liberate me from the mediocrity of a stagnant sound mind.

Where's The Funny Brownie?

"There is nothing concealed that will not be disclosed, or hidden that will not be made known" (Luke 12:2)

A neighborhood parent of a special education student was upset that her son was discharged without notice from his charter high school. Now Jericho Walls Charter High School was like a fortress unto itself. The founder, Director Dr. Dominique Recta , was described by the school's neighborhood to be like the controlling sinister character Han from the classic movie Enter the Dragon. Under no circumstances were the parents allowed into the school building without having an advance appointment. Even if it was an emergency, parents were not allowed to enter the building nor even speak directly to the director without a granted appointment. There also was a pattern of students from needy families being expelled and dismissed abruptly without proper due process from this financial grant grubbing machine of an institution.

Dear Tabla,
After several attempts I was finally allowed an audience to meet with the principal Dr. Dominique Recta as long I didn't bring the overwhelmed parent and allegedly problematic student. I was escorted by school security upstairs via a special elevator which according to posted signs was designated to be exclusively used by the director. As the elevator doors opened I could see her sitting at the end of a long majestic table. I noticed sitting around her faces of religious, political and highly influential personalities. The administration reported that the teen brought and sold weed brownies in the school's premises . He was discharged on the basis that the school had a selective tainted zero tolerance policy. This was repeatedly stated as they interjected, cutting me off whenever I attempted to speak on behalf of the family. The director adorned her zero tolerance stance with scripture references of what is righteous with her cloud of witnesses saying their affirming amens, hallelujah and 'just doing the

right thing for the people'. Any seeds of reasonable compassion I could barely cast just fell on indifferent stony hearts, left for a murder of well fed crows to eat.

As I was leaving the school director contemptuously commented that she has heard that I had a somewhat Columbo type of reputation amongst the religious community. I turned around and told her that I happen to be a ardent fan of the television show's character. I went on to give her a tidbit regarding the detective character as the actor Peter Falk explained him in an interview. The actor explained that in his development of the Colombo character, he did not necessarily make him conniving and astute, but rather just very obsessive with details that may not be important to other investigators. His obsessiveness had him let clues themselves lead the way, not being dissuaded by his more sophisticated opponents. Then in a Colombo like fashion I rubbed the top of my head in a circling fashion seven times and then proceeded to ask her in the fictional homicide detective's voice "Just one more thing, if you please". She in the others laughed and then appeared startled when I asked the director whatever happened to the funny brownies the boy had been accused of bringing into the school. She then inquired what I meant and I explained that although schools had a zero tolerance for students bringing in illegal substances, the schools then had a city mandated obligation to report it to law-enforcement as well as surrender the item. There was a moment of silence as I stepped out and told them "I'm sure you will do the right thing". Shortly after the parent and student contacted me and while praising God informed me that the young man was allowed to come back into the school. They asked me how I was able to convince the school. As I rubbed my hair seven times I just told them that I had asked the administration to do the right thing just as I asked the parent and student to do the right thing. In remorseful and repentant fashion they softly confessed that the mother was being treated for cancer and the student had gotten into her medical marijuana.

"Now the gates of Jericho were securely barred because of the Israelites. No one went out and no one came in....On the seventh day, the Israelites got up at daybreak and marched around the city seven times ... they shouted, and at the sound of the trumpet, when the men gave a loud shout, the Jericho wall collapsed; so everyone charged straight in, and they took the city."
-Joshua Chapter 6-

110

HISSKAMASHONDA QUIQUE

"And we know that in all things God works for the good of those who love him, who have been called according to his purpose"
(Romans 8:28)

Raja was invited to church by a Pastor Sylvia, she wanted him to participate in an intervention involving a young man,who was Quique, abusing drugs and his concerned family members. Pastor Sylvia was a bit more progressive when it came to her dress code. She actually had some highlighted hair, light make up and even at times wore some modest jewelry. There were some of the older members that took issue with that. Especially Profeta who may have been making some moves to take over leadership. Raja came late to the church during their evening mid week service and sat in the back. That week he had been growing a goatee which in many of the more rigid dress coded Pentecostal churches was frowned upon at that time. There was a middle-age lady known as Profeta who took notice of Raja. She passed up and down the aisles several times while looking me from head to toe and shaking her head. As she walked up to the front, one of the church members who appeared to be a member of the OSC whispered something into her ear. Profeta then made a "oh" facial gesture. During the church's moment of collective intercessory prayer, she began to speak loudly in tongues walking toward Raja and then prophesying over him in a stern manner. It did not go well.

Dear Tabla,
Last week Pastora Sylvia Yatusabes shared about a family needing assistance regarding a substance-abuse issue. The family being new members to her church had shared how their older son relapsed. There was going to be a family intervention in the pastor's office after their evening church service. Pastor Sylvia was a very innovative and

trailblazing minister. An example of that is the time many churches in that area were protesting against a bar that had opened there. Not jumping on the protesting parade, Pastora Sylvia had approached the bar owner making a proposition. The owner had agreed to call her and then she would call a couple of her deacons whenever the bar needed one of their heavily intoxicated customers safely driven or escorted home. This rather unorthodox arrangement did not sit well with many of the older folks of Sylvia's church, especially with Profeta. Yet there were many family members of these escorted folk that were grateful to Pastora Sylvia. This new family was one of them. They came to her church seeking assistance for their son Quique (Spanish common nickname for Enrique).

Arriving a bit tardy to the church service I opted to sit by the back pews, as to not be a distraction to the congregants there. There was a lady there, which I later found out to be named Profeta, walking up and down the aisles while checking me out. Profeta I also learned has been a long time member at the church and was a self proclaimed prophet. Someone in the front of their sanctuary had whispered something into her ear. Then she slowly started walking toward me while speaking in tongues at an escalating volume: "HISSKAMASHONDA!!!…Quique Quique Quique, I The Lord have known you since birth…. HISSKAMASHONDA!!!Quique Quique Quique…HISSKAMASHONDA!!!" I looked over to Pastora Sylvia and made some gestures to her as to ask her what the heck is happening here. She smiled and looked back at me with a she's one of my church headaches. Profeta continued in an even higher volume and tone "Quique Quique Quique HISSKAMASHONDA!!!" Until she reached me and laid hands over me. I responded by leaning over and whispering in Profeta ear "Sister, I am not Quique". Profeta then opened up one eye "You are not Quique?" I responded "No Lord, I am not Quique. I'm

113

Pastor Raja ". Then, in an almost Lily Tomlin voice, Profeta blurted, "Oh, never mind". Then she continued her HISSKAMASHONDA speaking in tongues going from a loud volume to a low volume Profeta moved away walking toward the restroom area ..."HISss comma ...." . And the Honda left in a whimper. Apparently when she saw me sitting in the back with my jeans and ungodly goatee, she mistook me for Quique who she had never met. I think that Profeta possibly wanted to perform some sort of deliverance because she placed little credence that the Lord may possibly approve of an intervention approach. Some congregants sitting near me that evening found it humorous. Others sitting not within ear shot away found this transaction, like her signature tongues, somewhat incomprehensible. A bit later in Pastor Sylvia's office the intervention meeting with Quique and his family members was very productive. A rather shaken Quique accepted the proposed inpatient program I recommended and helped him get into. Somehow he interpreted Profeta's earlier encounter with me as the Lord giving me instructions as to what to recommend for Quique. Pastora Yatusabes and I just ran with it.

Choking on Lying Mammon

Keep your lives free from the love of money and be content with what you have, because God has said, "Never will I leave you; never will I forsake you." (Hebrews 13:5)

Raja prayerful sought God's wisdom regarding collaborating with someone who had become very successful with nonprofit grants. Benició was a former drug addicted thug, who started from very humble beginnings, now had a thriving and fast paced growing organization. He had been soliciting many small churches with attractive propositions. It was presented as a way to funnel monies from repentant moguls to the underserved communities with ecclesiastical entities receiving blessed hefty finder's fees. Benició presented this as a theocratic strategy benefiting churches in disenfranchised impoverished areas. He appeared to be well versed in liberation theological jargon. Raja himself had come to believe through some personal experiences and studied sociological theories, that there were wealthy institutions that intentionally engineered ways to shortchange the less financially successful. He also understood that oppression can be exercised by any socioeconomic group. One time Raja was instrumental in unmasking a big time religious figure who turned out to be a slum lord. This slum lord had been hiring street thugs to harass and terrorize tenants. Now a few years later everything successful Benició proposed sounded as an answered prayer for the needs of small local storefront churches, including Raja's church. Still an uneasy Raja tried to confer with some of the other neighboring clergy on board with the Benició blessing. They all told Raja that he should just power pray past his reserved mental clutter of anxieties and not look at the Lord's gift horse in the mouth. A year later flash news stories broke out that Benició was arrested for intentionally laundering monies for unsavory characters. Suddenly any clergy that got involved with Benició organization began frantically calling Raja seeking his counsel. They were hoping against hope to find a sure fire way to distance themselves from Benició.

Dear Tabla,

Another crazy divine appointed day. Last year I prayerfully gave Benició a hard pass to his invitation to join his collective of ministers benefiting from his nonprofit organization. Before making the decision to decline joining them, I visited Pastor Custodio's church. I occasionally visit the old preacher's small church to listen to his sermons for inspiration and insight. That evening Pastor Custodio preached about the devil's modality of seducing. He then used a classic illustration about a lustful billionaire and a beautiful moral woman. The sexualized mogul proposed that he would give her millions of dollars so she could help others if she slept with him once. She thought about how this opportunity would fund her dreams of a world wide ministry to the needy. The next morning after his appetite for a beautiful young virgin was satisfied, he gave her $10. Outraged she exclaimed 'What do you think I am?'. He replied 'We've already established what you are. What we now have to settle on is a price'. Pastor Custodio concluded the sermon with Don't let the Evil One misguide you with false and cunning hype. Stay sober through the True Redeemer. Well, I took that as a sign not to go forth with joining Benició's organization. Turned out that the supposedly God's gift horse turned out to be a Trojan horse from the lying Spirit of Mammon. My ministerial peers, unlike me, who joined the organization called me expressing worry about the reputation of their ministries and extreme anger toward Benició. They seemed to think I would I TOLD YOU SO slap them silly. They bitterly anguished that they were seduced by a man from a spiritual breed described in scripture such as St. Paul's warning : 'But those who desire to be rich fall into temptation and a snare, and into many foolish and harmful lusts which drown men in destruction and perdition. For the love of money is a root of all kinds of evil, for which some have strayed from the faith in their greediness, and pierced *themselves through with many sorrows!' When I sat in our living room with Tesoro, I shared with her how relieved I was that I got guidance through Pastor Custodio's sermon illustration. Then my precious Tesoro threw a monkey wrench into how I processed the moment. She suggested that I should consider that it was Benició who was first duped by the Father of Lies in this case. She reminded me of the times I myself had tapped into Benició's brain and resources way before he became a successful CEO. The many times, prior to this sad phase of his life, he had come through to help members of our church who were in desperate need..Now I need to be there for him at his worse time. To be there for Benició not to just to be another enabling yes man or nor a come back bigger and better public relations promoter, but there as a 'Hesed' presence. A redemptive love in the midst of ugly consequences.*

Santa's Panties

"For God is not the author of confusion, but of peace, as in all churches of the saints." (1 Corinthians 14:33)

Raja was under the weather and under bed covers during one winter holiday. He received an urgent call from an elder from another church. The pastor of that church was away, taking care of a family emergency in his native island of Puerto Rico. The pastor has left Deaconess Daniela in charge of the church during his absence. There was a scandal that broke out at the church involving the jealous husband of one of the members. He was searching for a 16-year-old church member who he claimed had made sexual advances toward his wife. Tesoro took the call and persuaded Raja to let her go and take care of the situation. This being that she had a good community rapport with the family of the enraged violent jealous man.

Dear Tabla,

A couple of days ago I received an urgent call from Deaconess Daniela regarding a dangerous situation at her church. Although she was covering for her pastor that was away, the Deaconess felt that this situation was way over her head. Apparently there was a gun toting angry man from the neighborhood seeking to do harm to one of their teenage church members. Teenage Choco was known to be a very respectable young man with no history of inappropriate behaviors. He led the church youth group and often volunteered to help senior citizens in the vicinity. Choco was also a honor roll high school student as well as a diehard student of the Bible. Manny was known to be a big strong man known for his trigger line explosive anger. His wife Tina was a very sweet and attractive young woman who started attending church. My dear wife Tesoro had developed a good rapport with this particular family, being that she had advocated and helped them out from dyer situations. After calming Manny down, Tesoro was able to arrange a sit down with him, his *lovely wife Tina, Deaconess Daniela, a terrified Choco and his mother . At the meeting Manny pulled out a gift box of women's panties claiming that this was a gift that Choco had given his wife. Choco exclaimed "What !!", Then looked at his mother. ESCÁNDALO (Scandalous!!) A set of seven large assorted colored panties each embroiled with the day of the week. That's what Choco's mom purchased for him when he gave her money to shop for him for the Intercambió de Regalo (gift exchange)- a Secret Santa type of holiday event at the small Spanish Pentecostal church. He asked his mom for assistance being that he wasn't sure what to get his Secret Santa lady person. This was a fun activity where church members voluntarily participated in. They would pass around an offering basket with folded scraps of paper. Each piece of paper has the name of a participating member. Whatever name you got out of the basket you were to secretly purchased a holiday gift not exceeding $15. Unbeknownst to Choco, his mother had purchased these fancy undergarments for his Secret Santa victim. It did not occur to her how this would be an most unsuitable gift for a teenage young man to give to a married woman. Choco's mother reportedly became embarrassed and deeply apologized to the lovely Tina, the angry Manny, Deaconess Daniela and especially to Choco. Tesoro then laughingly pulled the infamous box of weekday customized panties as she completed her report to me. Apparently both parties at the meeting agreed to give Tesoro the secret Santa gift as a thank you for her help in clarifying the matter. My slender and beautiful Tesoro buried her new treasure in the bedroom closet to use in the future when or if ever she was granted the opportunity to fit into an even more shapely size large. I secretly look forward to that day. Maranatha ....but...Please do not return quickly Lord Jesus.*

Photoshopping Juanmarco

"Whoever conceals his transgressions will not prosper, but he who confesses and forsakes them will obtain mercy" (Proverbs 28:13)

Rev. Juanmarco was someone who Raja had admired for years. He had located from a southern state to our urban city and pioneered an admirable model church. Sister Eva was a new member at trailblazer Pastora Sylvia Yatusabes' church and had a history of nitty gritty social advocacy for our underserved communities. As Sylvia and Raja were organizing a small local conference, Doctora Eva Marx de Cristo learned that Juanmarco would be one of the presenters. Eva then venomously expressed that she had no respect for him. On the day of the conference Eva appeared strangely calm at the presence of Juanmarco. But soon after we moved away from the eye of the potentially brewing storm, we were suddenly sucked into the manifested storm. Rev. Juanmarco suddenly and explosively began yelling at Eva. He appeared very outraged as he turned over a table of brochures that was situated near his display.

Dear Tabla,

Today we we underwent a little demonic fart of sorts as we went about to make God's Kingdom better. I guess that effort could become more putrid within any delusions that the Lord really needs our cutting edge logistics. Previously Pastora Sylvia Yatusabes approached me to assist her regarding a desire in her heart to bring more affordable and relevant leadership training to local pastors. It was an honor to be invited to join her in organizing this event. Clergy from seemly successful urban based ministries were invited to be headline speakers, sharing insights from their own church growth. Now weeks ago Dr. Eva Marx de Cristo was very, to say the least, displeased when she learned that Pastor Juanmarco would be one of the main speakers. We were at a loss as to why such a well centered eloquent advocate of the downtrodden would just incoherently grumble about the man. We would have attributed it to Eva just somehow being envious of him, but that conclusion would have not made sense. She was a new Christ follower and never made any claims nor interest in any type of formal ministry. It was usual in many Spanish Pentecostal churches for new believers to claim, be guided or misguided to believe they had some grandeur calling. That is, a spectacular spotlight level formal ministry. Eva had no such designs. She humbly came to the Lord after a strong in your face approach to giving voice to the voiceless in many of our oppressed communities. Eva's surrender to Jesus was more of a surrender of her radical fire for social equity in exchange for an even more powerful fire. A fire accompanied by a new teachable personal spirit in God's holy written word.

As a teen, I had the joy of attending some of Juanmarco' dynamic bible studies. At that time the new pastor that came from another part of the country seemed to relate well to both churched and unchurched kids. He had the resources to expose street kids to better life perspectives. Juanmarco also empathized with disenchanted church raised youths, offering them nicely equipped opportunities to spread their ministering wings inside the safe space of his newly acquired church building. So it was a wonder why these two wonderful folks in my life had such a tremendous personality crash. The crashing sound of Eva's brochure table and Juanmarco yelling 'How Dare You!!' at her, was not necessarily part of a planned conference intermission. But Pastora Sylvia and I were grateful to God that at least it happened at the intermission. Eva had been asking for the gift of tongues, but today she was utilizing her old life's street French....laughing and telling Juanmarco "How do you @#%#ing like that?!!!" Sylvia and I grabbed and rushed these two into the pastor's office with the aide of a couple volunteers from a community football team.

In the office Pastora Sylvia laid down the law for a civil mediation between the two children of God who appeared to be emerging hooligans in of all places her first dream conference. Juanmarco claimed that Eva had been harassing him for the past few months regarding one of his promotional brochures. Unlike many of the conventional storefront churches in the city, his church was a missions church. That is a church that gets funding from by a large financially robust religious denomination in order to be and remain planted in what they have identified as a needy area. The ministers of such churches then go around the nation for a short period once a year making presentations of their urban missions work and soliciting continual funding. This includes slide presentations, videos, dynamic tearjerking stories of lives that have been touched and transformed by their work. Apparently Eva came across one of such brochures which were produced at a print shop owned by one of her acquaintances. She was more than bothered that the pictures in this particular promotional literature were from urban areas where Juanmarco' church wasn't located at nor had any significant interactions with. She found this to be false advertisement in order for his church to receive continued high funding as well as impressive equipments. Juanmarco then reported that he attempted to explain how this type of advertisement was not necessarily deceptive but Eva was not having any of that rationale. He then done cut her off from having any communications with him nor with his church whose staff were instructed not to accept any messages or visits from her. Juanmarco reported that for a short period of time Eva ceased pursuing the heated matter. Now at the convention he noticed a small table near his promotional table. It was Eva's a little table with brochures with content he found very insulting. The pamphlet had a picture of his son with an unflattering narrative. At that point I asked to see this item. Yep, there it was. It was a picture of

Juanmarco Junior taken off social media. It was photoshopped to look like the world famous side street NYC Times Square guitar playing-singing naked cowboy raising funds. Eva acknowledge having printed that pamphlet and setting the little table next to Juanmarco's promotional display. We asked her why she would do such a classless thing. Then she pulled out a glossy newsletter from Juanmarco's ministry. There was a bloated article regarding his ministry reaching out to gang members and notorious drug dealers. Within the article there was a picture of Juanmarco's arm around Eva's son Evan. It was a picture that was taken during a Bible study conducted for young Christian leaders. The way that the picture was cropped in the article, would give readers the impression that he was one of the young criminals Juanmarco' ministry had reached.Eva tearfully said through grinding teeth that her son is an honor student that never lived such a life and that seeing that newsletter was the last straw that broke her heart and any patience. Especially when she a single parent, like many parents from the neighborhood, fought tooth and nail to keep her son on a path for a bright future. Eva was hoping that her stunt would trigger some kind of emotional intelligent aha moment in Juanmarco' psyche. I felt quite disappointed that Pastor Juanmarco wasn't quite processing Eva's pain. Sadly what surfaced was that he was more invested in changing the narrative to favor the idea of doing what it takes to build a kingdom. So the resulting dispute between us three and Juanmarco was so sharp that we parted company. We hope that some day we may reconcile like Saint Paul and St. John Mark did....even though both biblical saints weren't hellbent on building a costly and highly promoted empire.

Doc DM & The Lord of the Dance

"Let them praise his name with dancingand make music to him with timbrel and harp"(Psalm 149:3)

Dr. Bishop Dave Mohamed (nicknamed Doc DM) had a large congregation consisting of folks that were raised in very conservative Pentecostal churches as well as those with a non-church background. He was the love product of a Muslim father and Jewish mother. In his early teens during the 60s he began experimenting with mind altering substances. He became lost in the streets using any thing that would alter his consciousness, including sniffing glue. One afternoon there was a open-air street evangelistic service. A little amused during a brief lucid moment he approached the proselyting event. Running through his pockets he realized that had he ran out of bamboo paper and I asked one of the older women giving out gospel tracts for one of them. He rolled up his weed using the tract and began to light up and puff. Then he saw the smoke form words in front of him. There written in midair in a type of Spanglish but a blend of Hebrew and Arabic was a message about a God who so loved him and that did want him to perish any longer. Doc DM asked the lady who was distributing literature for prayer. She touched his shoulder and began praying in what he thought at first was celestial tongues. It turns out that she enjoyed praying in a Castilian Spanish poetic style whenever she was moved by anything or moment she thought was God sent. He went on to enroll in a faith based rehabilitation program and received much support from the Spanish Pentecostal church. Once he completed his program the church offered him a custodial job which he was grateful for. There he was discipled and as well as schooled in ministerial studies by a near African-American seminary. Doc DM then started a ministry from scratch with the church and the seminaries blessing. Over the years his pioneered church grew immensely. But something disturbing recently started causing older members from his congregation to leave. Rumors going around nearby religious communities was that he was turning his church into some sort of rowdy disco dancing club. One of the older members of Raja's church was concerned that their son, daughter-in-law and children were caught up in this cultic type of heretic environment. Another concern was that the manifestations were akin to the historic dangerous dance mania epidemics that appeared centuries ago across mainline Europe. Raja's older church member pleaded him to please go visit the church and retrieve the family for some cult deprogramming.

Querida Tabla,
Today what's a rather interesting stealth assignment into a potential Jonestown situation. There were alarming stories traveling through the doctrinally correct grapevine that a sinister activity was occurring inside Dr. Dave Mohamed's church. As I shook off the shared anxieties I came into the sanctuary with an open mind and heart still guarded with The sword of Truth. After listening to the powerful message delivered by a true master wordsmith the church started an end of the service worship time. My skin was invaded by goosebumps as I heard young voices rushing down the aisle praising Allah, Yeshua , Jehová and dancing. Doc DM invited more children to come and they came dancing while holding hands. Then he invited the elderly and they came and danced like children. And then the handicapped were invited to come and dance. So there they were folks of different ethnic groups, backgrounds and disabilities dancing. Children dancing in circles holding hands. Then I saw Doc DM take off his blazer , take off his necktie, unbutton his neck buttons and his heavy set body flew up from the elevated pulpit landed one knee on the floor and opposite arm extended behind him like a superhero. I was in awe as I watched him dance reckless and gracefully while looking up toward a greater awe. Something bigger than my heart and lungs felt like it would joyfully explode. As I stepped out of the church I saw some of the brothers

and sisters that had conveyed to me their concerns regarding Doc DM new directions. They asked my opinion regarding the scandalous dancing. I told them that I was still processing but I had to tell them that I felt emotionally uplifted. Also impressive was that nothing in their sanctuary needed picking up or repaired, unlike some churches I had visited where it seem gigantic Beyblade's destructively spun through. Regarding their concerns about Allah being allowed into the Lord's temple. They seem to be unaware of the history of the name. It's a Arabic generic word , same way the English word God is a generic word for deity. Allah was used ages before Islam came into the scene. Then I used the example of the Spanish word Dios. Dios isn't necessarily an evil word nor a counterfeit God just because it is used by thousands of Hispanic/Latino drug cartel members. It was an unfortunate comparison but I think they got the point. Anyways, tonight Tesoro got up and caught me dancing while singing Spanish Pentecostal ballads to God. I told her how I was so sleeplessly moved from what I witnessed that I just had to get to the living room for some consecrated privacy. As Tesoro started to go to bed, I asked if she would like to join me in my late night worship dance. She turned around looking at me and started making some break dance moves and spitting out some hip-hop lyrics which she knows I personally loathe. Then she proceeded going back to bed and I thought, "You know Lord? She did sound kinda good".

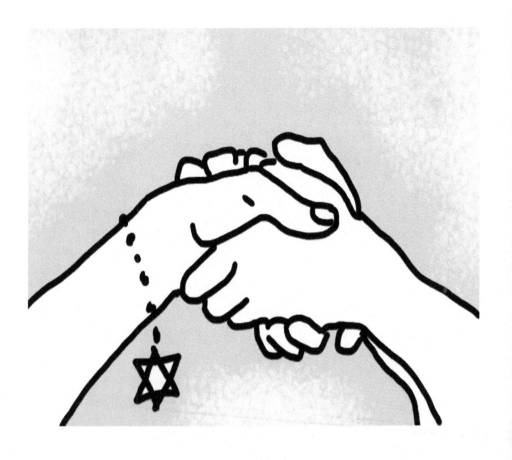

Lady Rabbi in the House

"I will bless those who bless you, and him who dishonors you I will curse, and in you all the families of the earth shall be blessed."
(Genesis 12:3)

The local trabajo personal band was worried about a Spanish Pentecostal family from downtown Harlem that have not been seen in a while. Trabajo personal meaning personal work was the duty of church members to personally go to homes near their church area, knock on doors, invite families to the church and share the gospel. This activity was not limited to individual churches. Many Christians from different fellowships would hit high traffic places to spread the good news. They also enjoy socially interacting with members of different congregations. Now the family in the center of concern was Brother Justino , Sister Sarai and her two adult daughters Esperanza and Promesa who were known to hop from church to church. They were reported to be a rather bizarre, awkward and yet friendly family. It was rumored that the father was involved in some sort of domestic violence and have been keeping them hostage.

Dear Tabla,
Today I accompanied Sister Rosa to the household of the hostage family. Rosa told me that she had learned that when Brother Justino left from work he secured the apartment door in a manner his wife and daughters would not step out. On his days off he would escort them to and from a nearby park. Sister Sarai had managed to be able to open the door and let Rosa in for a brief time of fellowship during the weekday. But she had become very uncomfortable and shaken during the visits. Rosa and the band requested my assessment. I was able to visit the household briefly thanks to Rosa's introduction. Although I could not pinpoint what disturbed me regarding this friendly family, I was spooked by Rosa's conclusion. She had sized up the situation of there being some paranormal satanic presence invading this family's soul. While Rosa began organizing her social media cell phone documentary crew, I went ahead

and did what was considered to be quite an unorthodox move among many of my peers. I called my friend Rabbi Donna. Donna was a highly regarded clergy from a nearby small reform synagogue. Like me, she was a bi-vocational clergy where the majority of her salary came from the secular field. She loved leading her congregation in biblical studies, ethical values as well as worship. Donna was also a well respected psychiatrist. When I described the situation to her she agreed without hesitation to come with me to observe and informally assess the family. I decided to have a promising exorcist Rosa left out of this venture. When I rang the doorbell Sister Sarai recognized me and allowed me and Donna into the apartment. We were invited to sit in the living room while the girls prepared and offered us hot beverages and pastries. Sarai engaged me in Spanish, a language which Donna had little mastery of. She looked at Donna who was wearing earrings, light and makeup and casual pants. I could somewhat gauge the sister's upcoming question. "Is she a Christian?", before I could reply Donna asked me what the Sarai was saying. I translated and Donna replied while looking at the sister "No, I am Jewish". The sister then replied "Judía?" The girls chimed in "El pueblo de Dios". The mother then looked at her girls and affirmed "Sí, el pueblo de Dios". All three gleefully repeated and broke out singing. Donna then looked at me and asked what the commotion was about and I interpreted that they had said "the Jews - God's people". I briefly explained to the rabbi that this is often what is pressed about the Jewish people in Spanish Pentecostal churches. The rabbi sat and appeared quite moved as the family began to sing some of the Spanish psalm themed songs regarding Israel and Jerusalem. Afterward Donna engaged them and they happily responded to simple questions. They caressed the rabbi's hands, bidding us shalom and inviting Donna back. Donna expressed being more than pleasantly surprised at their reception of her as opposed to antisemitic resistance. Dr. Donna then explained to me that Sarai and the *girls were displaying signs of schizophrenia. It was possible that Justino was doing his best to keep his family safe. There needed to be some sort of orientation provided so the family could receive outpatient supportive services. Tesoro was there when I passed this info to an apprehensive leadership of the church they currently attended. I sighed at this roadblock and a fired up Tesoro rubbed my back, telling me "In Jesus name, I'll take it from here mi dulce del corazón" (my sweet heart). Tesoro joined forces with Donna and intercepted Justino one day when he was returning home. Then disaster happened. The horror of any male centered expectation of women getting it wrong .... a fascinated Justino listened intently to a member of el pueblo de Dios. Enjoying learning Hebrew and Yiddish words while giving up his sweet spot of ignorance, he was persuaded to receive clinical support for the family. B'ezrat Hashem (with G-d's help).*

He Said She Said Call 911

"Do not repay anyone evil for evil. Be careful to do what is right in the eyes of everyone. If it is possible, as far as it depends on you, live at peace with everyone" (Romans 12:17-18)

There was an unfortunate incident that occurred during a street evangelistic open-air meeting. It was reported that a pastor was assaulted and injured. He was now hospitalized and the suspect was arrested but then released without bail. Part of the religious community credited Satan for the vicious attack. The neighborhood swore that the suspect, although known at times to be rowdy, was not responsible for the well known pastor's critical condition. There were OSC fervent prayer meetings. Some supplicating the Lord for the pastor's full health recovery. Others were calling down God's wrath upon the non-church infidel. Others were praying for community healing. Parties of both religious and non-religious factions requested Raja's involvement.

Dear Tablita,

Another inconvenient divine assignment was bestowed upon me last week. A somewhat messy one. Pastór Sancho is infamously known in church circles as being from the dictator school of leadership. He plans events, delegated duties and last-minute micromanaged and strip modified the laborious work of his submissive volunteers. Now it was the scheduled season for souls to be saved with the aid of city permits to close off streets and for blasting loud speakers. Now Chacón is a regular in the local scenery. This soul was a colorful and voicetrous character with an extra over the top persona who is always in the street. It is unclear whether this person is actually homeless or is some trust fund adult baby from an affluent family that loves to be bumming in this New York City poor neighborhood. Chacón often appears colorfully disheveled and impaired only to break out reciting beautiful poetry as well as charmingly singing themes relevant to whatever was transpiring at the moment in the area. Pastór Sancho took a huge dislike to Chacón who he believed was there to ruin the minds of impressional youngsters. Now, trying to gather and assess details of the brutal incident the past two days was quite a chaotic task. Still dizzy from my novice investigation I got home to enjoy relaxing quality time with my much better half. We spoke about our day with fuming sounds, giggles and laughter. Tesoro shared a messenger communication she received from one of her Facebook friends living in the Dominican Republic. Alma was an old diehard seeker of dream interpreters. I'm not too keen on this obsession. But I thought I would get a kick out of listening to an unsolved dream this evening. Tesoro began reading Alma's dream to me:

Anoche soñé que mientras pasaba vecindad extraña, observé un culto evangélico al aire libre. Una señora de edad empezó orar sobre un ser necesitado que pidió la oración. Entonces una persona sobre peso , que aparentemente era el pastor, interrumpió a la señora y le dijo que no ore por el ser por que los demonios que él tenía sólo salían con mucha ayuno y oración. La pobre alma escuchó eso y respondió, "Tu panza es lo que necesita salir con mucho ayuno y oración gordinflón!!"

Translation-
Last night I dreamed that while I was passing by a strange neighborhood, I observed an open air evangelical service. An older lady began to pray for a person in need who asked for prayer. Then an overweight person, who apparently was the pastor, interrupted the lady and told her not to pray for the poor soul because the demons he had only came out with a lot of fasting and prayer. The poor soul heard that and replied, "Your belly is what needs to come out with lots of fasting and praying you fat slob!!"

My loftiness suddenly froze like a deer stunned still by a car's high beam lights. I looked up beyond the ceiling thinking "Could this be?". After a moment I called a couple of reserved believers who witnessed the catastrophic event and told them the dream from a far away land. They broke down and gave me first hand details that were classified, away from common public knowledge, for the sake of their ministries. It turned out that Chacon was touched emotionally by one of the older lady's singing. He/She approached her requesting prayer. In the midst of a compassionate prayer, Pastor Sancho abruptly and forcefully removed the aging hands off Chacon. He scolded the lady telling her that 'inhuman' was full of demonic armies and needed a transforming full fledged exorcism. Not a Roman Catholic ritualistic one, but a powerful prayer and fast empowered iron clad deliverance. Chacon then rapid fired scriptures at Sancho about how gluttony was also a sin, and how the pastor physically showcased a sloppy obese need for serious fasting. That he had to be a better caretaker of the body temple God loaned him. Suddenly the minister verbally expressing outrage, fell to the ground...courtesy of an overdue cardiac arrest. His church ministers panicked into loud prayers and laying hands on Sancho. Chacon yelled STAY CALM FOLKS & SOMEONE CALL 911 , pushed them aside and began doing CPR chest compressions until EMS arrived. Long story short, despite what they thought, he/she saved Sancho's life. I visited Pastor Sancho at the hospital where he was recovering well. He had been declining visits from Chacon and began giving me his customized version of what happened. I cut his tall tale short by telling him I knew what I believed to be the genuine storyline. Then I shamefully told him a borderline white lie, that being that I truly believed that he was better than a selfish soul that would stubbornly not acknowledge Chacon's heroism. I took advantage of what I perceived to be a fracture line in his bloated ego and had he receive a FaceTime phone convo with his guardian angel. In an anemic attempt of a thank you he told Chacon that Father God loved him/her and wanted the best for him/her. After a brief silence chacon told Sancho that all lives are precious and she-he *believed that his children would have been devastated if he had perished due to poor self care. Later in a conversation with Chacon I learned that he – she was actually born a biological female and was still a biological female. Her bizarre appearance was due to a fake medical doctor injecting her with a hardening substance instead of silicone in the past. I was saddened by the story when she then told me to "Cheer up guy, it could have been worse. Pastor Sancho could have needed mouth-to-mouth resuscitation..."*

UNDERWATER Comicstrip Rest Stop For Your Eyes ;)

Feeling a little frustrated over situations that should have been resolved easily Raja prayed and turned to newspaper funnies. Once in a while Raja would looked through his collection of cartoon strip drafts created back in the 80s by his friend Jeffrey Cortez AKA PJeff. His buddy would draw these and send them to his close circle of friends in the ministry. He did this as a relaxing and enjoyable exercise as he himself reflected on his own journey as a Bivocational minister. The title of the unpublished yet copyrighted strip was UNDERWATER and the central theme was around the tug-of-war of interpersonal relationships and the very plight of social adjustments.

Two of his cartoon characters was Salm and Rev. Pyro-N-Brimstone. Rev. Pyro-N-Brimstone is the clergy that prefers dealing with a fishing rod than dealing with people. Not exactly a fisher of souls, he prefers conjuring up fish stories than sermons. His highest ambition is to catch Salm the legend. Salm The salmon who is a retired legend among fishermen. There are rumors to the effect that psalm was formally a human that sought the life of a fish yet not willing to give up his talented hands for fins. He is a jacque of all fine arts, yet maestro of none. There is one thing he has mastered – the undisciplined life of a procrastinator. Gabbs the clam is the world experienced senior citizen. Seeking someone to share his well earned wisdom with or at least company. Salm constant ignoring of Gabbs' attempts at conversation, actually deprive the salmon of some enriching know how. Seaweed: Is it animal, mineral or vegetable? This may be everyone's question concerning seaweed. But that's OK. He really knows who and what he is and that is all that counts to him. For some reason Salm is always nagging him with advice and brow beating.

154

Dialing God The Hitman

"The heart is deceitful above all things and beyond cure. Who can understand it?" (Jeremiah 17:9)

Brother Helio came to Raja with a concerning report. The OSC had invited a rising popular power couple whose ministry were supposed to teach believers the deeper secrets of the Bible. They taught that believers should not be limited to the written scriptures and had sovereign authority to speak realities into existence in the same manner that God himself created the universe. When the couple learned that Raja would be attending one of their seminars they became agitated. The couple then took control of the prayer service, pressuring and manipulating the group to conduct spiritual warfare against Raja. The strange mantra that they were using was "Raja, in Jesus name I command you to forget". Helio came with me to confront these menacing strangers raising hostilities against me. I came into one of the OSC centers where they were. When we saw each other my spirit aflame I called them out by their first names (their first names weren't in their brochures). I warned them against any further slanderous murder of my good name. They left town.

Dear Tabla,

Today I learned that there was some sort of spiritual warfare against my memory banks. At first I thought that Brother Helio was pulling my leg but the expression on his face negated that thought. There was a couple that were promoting themselves as high-level master teachers of the word of God. Which is not necessarily anything new, although concerning, to our classical and neo charismatic movements. In a nutshell it was a novel idea that God did not limit himself to giving us a written Holy Spirit inspired scriptures but believers can be anointed to speak new truths and revelations beyond the boundaries of scriptures. It turns out that the couple became very visibly agitated when they learned I was invited to preview their presentations as well as publications. They began to allege that I would not approve of their ministry based on them being a divorced couple. But that didn't make sense because I didn't know them let alone know their marriage status. Why would they launch a Prayer missile attack against my brain cells? This amusing news triggered my curiosity and my unquiet Spidey senses . Helio drove me over to the church were these two perched themselves. As I entered the circle where my name was being lifted up, the ardent clamor ceased when I called the leading pair by their first names. I recognized the couple. Dwayne and Carla. I knew them when the husband was single and the wife was married to somebody else.

A couple of decades ago I was new to El Tabernáculo Assemblies when I dropped out from bible college. Not being able to pay for my semester nor for the new academic year, I took time off to build up my finances. Returning to the Bronx I opted to leave my childhood church that resented my choosing and attending a non dress code ridden religious college. At my new accepting Pentecostal church I met Carla who was a young married woman who enjoyed intrusively prophesying over young adults. She tried that on me but I stopped her cold when I opened my bible to weigh and test her next patented God breathed words to me. That was a wet towel that kept her from trying that on me in the future. Like in my former church this church's youths would walk to their home together after a late weekday service. Carla would cling to them on the way attempting to awe them with her exclusive revelations about each of their futures. Some began replicating my open bible approach which deterred Carla from delivering them divinely customized purpose. One evening the group dwindled and I gentlemanly escorted Carla home. On the way he asked if I would join her in prayer regarding her call to ministry. She referred to my own journey in former ministerial training. Her loving husband, Dan, was an unbeliever who would be holding her back from her destiny. She had been praying that God would kill her devoted mate so that she could be unshackled to devote herself to grander things. I abruptly bided her good night, letting her slither the rest of her way home.

Years later I worked as a school intervention counselor servicing high risk students. Dwayne was a high school dean there who found out I was a believer and ordained minister. He felt that folks formerly trained for ministry were hindered spiritually because they were busy intellectualizing God's word. I suggested that he may possibly misreading folks that held the scriptures integrity instead of intellectualize it. Despite different views we bonded in good fellowship. One afternoon he asked if I would agree with him in a prayer requests that many shallow and immature Christian wouldn't understand. There were these married deacons , Andrew and Sherry in his church, whom he strongly felt that the wife should really be his. Dwayne had dated Sherry years ago but had broken up with her. Seeing how happy she was, Dwayne realized that he had messed up true God's preordained plan for him and her. Now he wanted to claim what Satan had unlawfully robbed him of. He informed me that Deacon Andrew was ill and the church were praying for his full recovery. Dwayne was praying that the Lord would quickly and mercifully take the deacon to glory. This way the enlightened dean could be free to comfort, court and marry the godly widow. I recommended him seek guidance from a seasoned mentor with clinical background. Now apparently his not receiving my Holy Ghost inspired piece of advise, he then ghosted me for the rest of my time working at that school's location.

Anyways, now I see them feverishly asking God, with a hijacked caravan of prayer warriors, to intercept and delete my not so flattering memory of them. I asked Carla if Dan was OK. She confirmed that he was all right. I asked Dwayne how the deacons were doing. He responded that they *were doing fine. I told them that I was glad that everyone was alive and kicking…. that including my keen recall (strained lighthearted comment). Now it is begrudgingly said, in many religious circles, that some denominations will not ordain divorced individuals but will ordain folks that have done prison time for murder. I exhorted the visiting dynamic duo to stop slandering me cause it could be just as bad as murder. Then again maybe murder was a feasible option in their rationale. In the end of it all Dwayne and Carla moved on. I just hope that someday they would find the exit out of the rabbit hole of believing that God's unmerited mercy gave them license to bypass His word.*

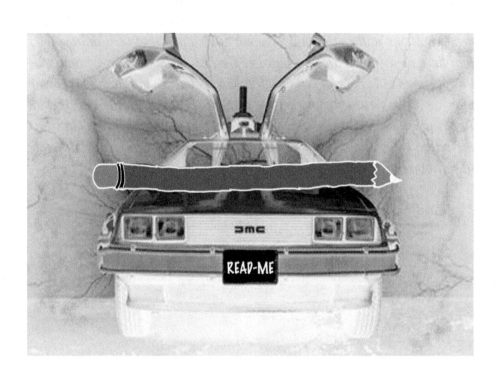

Holy Ghost Writer

"For we did not follow cleverly devised stories when we told you about the coming of our Lord Jesus Christ in power, but we were eyewitnesses of his majesty"
(2 Peter 1:16)

A religious Mega ministry celebrity came to the city planning a big event. He asked to meet with Raja and the circle of ministries from the area for a presentation. In the past he was a CEO of a major corporation that went bankrupt when investors sued. The product turned out to be a fancy techno prototype with its development seed monies spent on lavish lifestyles. Now he had reinvented himself as a dynamic personality in the televangelist realm. In the NYC meeting, Raja respectfully disagreed with the evangelist assumptions of his urban communities needs. The guest was eloquently dismissive of Raja's input, implying that Raja was ignorant of what was happening in the spiritual room of his community. To make his point he invited a poor down on his luck soul from the street into the meeting. After the first question the evangelist left in a big half and puff.

Hola Tabla,

Te va encantar este bochinche (You're gonna love this piece of gossip). A dear friend from out of town referred mega televangelist DeLorean De los Cielos to contact me so I could possibly help him set up a big event. My friend thought that the televangelist could benefit from picking my brain regarding his outreach methodology. DeLorean came wearing an expensive suit and other accessories worthy of a high end Hosanna greeting. He is a potentially likable character with the salesman's gift of gab. The brethren displayed an elaborate PowerPoint presentation. The premise of his outreach here was to get monies from well-to-do communities to help poor communities through his gizmos. Our poverty stricken communities according to him were being impacted by the presence of homeless individuals and families. He wanted us to provide him statistics showing that the primary reason for the homeless was substance abuse. I then countered, with as much respect I could muster, by asking him if he was familiar with our communities and the social elements impacting them.

He appeared just laser focused on getting drug abuser bloated statistics to justify his technology heavy solution. When he implied that the current poverty and substance-abuse problem in our communities were the unpaid bill of our local church, pioneer brother Garcia stopped him right there. The elderly pioneer confronted him for being ignorant of his neighborhood's status offering lavish vision casting designed to reinforce stereotypes with manipulated data. Pastor then quoted a famous American writer that once wrote that there were three types of lies - lies, damn lies and statistics. DeLorean appeared very defensive when I inquired what evidence he had for his hypothesis. He told us that it was a Holy Ghost prompting and then asked us to wait a moment. DeLorean then stepped out and invited Hemingway de Cervantes who was sitting near the church entrance. He escorted Hemingway (the neighborhood affectionately nicknamed him Hemmy) to the front and asked him to share his decline. He didn't like what Hemmy began sharing personal details. DeLorean abruptly interjected by offering Hemmy one of his famous and popular books. He told Hemingway that this book "the power of the Holy Ghost" will open your eyes and change your life. The evangelist then started to read a portion of his power packed inspirational book. Hemingway unexpectedly began quoting by memory long passages of it. Hemmy then indicated to the startled evangelist that he was very familiar with the literature because he actually wrote it. It turns out that Hemingway was a very well paid ghost writer for a lot of these personality driven ministries. What many fans of these popular religious organizations are unaware of is that the secret of their ability to frequently spit out books is their skilled anonymous writers. These writers get a flavor for the celebrity public speaking style then word craft a literary product. Some even research and write their sermons. Apparently ministerial businesses have given the Holy Spirit a backseat. Anyways, our dear discontented visiting orator rushed out, mounted on his other people's dime funded Jaguar and moved on to better wilderness.

NOTE: This chapter's epilogue: In the rush to leave this uncomfortable meeting, Hemingway left behind an expensive attaché case which contained a prototype of a Artificial Intelligent Sermon Maker possibly funded by faithful contributors.

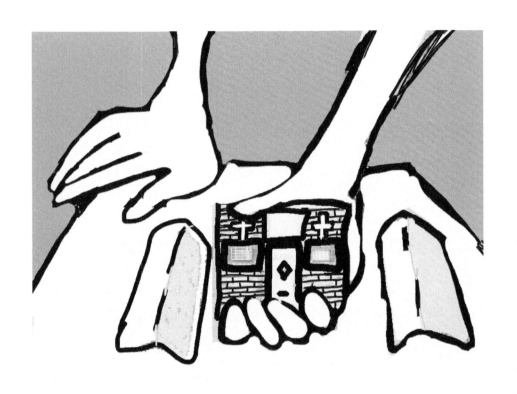

God Holds The Cards

"The Lord has made everything for its purpose, even the wicked for the day of trouble"(Proverbs 16:4)

Just as Raja's church became a little bit more consistent with their tithing and offerings, the owners of the storefront property gave the pastor the new lease rate effective in a couple of months. The amount which was almost triple the current price smelled like the beginning of a gentrification process in the neighborhood .There would be no amount of selling foods and other fundraising church activities that would be sustainable enough to keep up with this new lease rate. Hermana Atrevida, who had been saved one year, happily volunteered her Three Card Monte street hustle skills to raise funds. Raja gently explained that this tourist scam would not be ethical with her new life in Christ. He added that even if it was, it would not be sustainable nor legal. Later on Raja learned that the owners were had no intentions of leasing but were looking to sell their storefront property for a vast amount of money. The church leadership met and decided that they would definitely need to relocate, hopefully within the same neighborhood. Instead of leasing another storefront they set their eyes on a devastated property. Without Raja being aware one of the leaders were able to buy a foreclosed property from the city for one dollar. But it needed a lot of expensive work to be up to code. Another headache for the Pastor. He became a little anxious when he saw Sister Anti- Mavi Maria (our lottery guardian angel) lottery and Atrevida whispering and walking away. Raja then grabbed a brown paper bag, breathed into it to stop his hyperventilating and prayed that the Lord would take control of the whee......whirlwind.

Dearest Tabla,

Been managing my anxious racing thoughts the past few weeks with much prayer and some fasting. We have been looking for a new location in our area for the church to gather. Still, we simply did not have the funds or history of reliable income to afford the new lease rate for our current location. The cost of leases even for storefronts, has gone up. What was even more frustrating was finding out that the owners of our current site had used the lease increase as a ruse to get us out. They actually had put up the building for sale in what seemed to be a huge gentrification payday. What was additionally upsetting was that the week I was away vacationing with Tesoro, a couple of the church members had taken a donated vehicle and sold it. Others in leadership started a campaign to purchase a storefront building. They were working a plan to use monies raised to restore the building. Having a piece of property to them may have been a great idea, but all the financial responsibilities connected to it may have been above their understanding. This evening I attended a trustee meeting which Sister Anti- Mavi Maria and Atrevida requested. As I and the trustees exchanged heated words, ala the book of Acts, over the purchase of the heap barely recognizable as a building. This property ,although we did get it at a great price, would have been a a greater burden due to fines and penalties This realty even if it was cleaned out and such. As I came to my point, Maria and Atrevida smiled and handed over an envelope to us. We opened up the envelope we were taken aback to see a corporate check for a vast amount of money. It was made out to Atrevida and she had signed it over to the church. She announced that she and Maria were sure we now could afford to temporary meet at a leased storefront while being able to fully restore our new purchased property. My Holy Spirit Spider Senses began tingling and I inquired from Atrevida what she and Maria specifically do to persuade the corporation to give us such a generous amount of money for the sold vehicle.

It turned out that Atrevida went downtown to a Tinko's (a Office Print & Ship Services franchise) where she used her high school advertisement training to superimpose the logo of Howie Hughes Fox Realty

International (a Fortune 500 type of real estate developer) on a letterhead. Maria went to meet with Pillo & Pillos Inc. ,the owners of our leased property, and negotiated to purchase their property if they would allow her to put a fragment as a down payment. All parties were pleased and committed the deal to a typed and notarized contract. Soon after Maria had the contract, Atrevida mailed off a letter with the customized letterhead with the content expressing an interest in the property. When the owners, Pillo & Pillos Inc., received and read the letter, they thought that they had the potential of getting a lot more money for their property. They then contacted Maria offered her to refund the money she put down as a down payment. She then threatened to take them to court for breaking their contract. At the end, all parties agreed to a refund amounting to several times it's original amount. The ladies then told us "You see, we Pentecostals are not punks". Lord forgive me, at times I think of these sisters as thorns on my side that God gracefully refuses to relieve me from. I guess there will always be opportunities to allow God's Grace to devour those opportunities of when things go wrong. Shortly after, there was a national wide news release on these two companies. As of Pillo & Pillo Inc, they were mercilessly swallowed up by the bigger Howie Hughes Fox Realty company they sought out after not hearing from them....resistance was futile.

A Chancla Named Jesus

"The ultimate legacy of parents leave is how they dealt with their children when no one was looking."
(Somewhat Anonymous)

Raja enjoyed a small informal reunion with childhood friends from the church he was partly raised in. They told each other how their adult lives turned out. The little neighborhood diner filled with laughter as they updated each other with the latest news regarding certain colorful church personalities they knew. The friends paused in awe as they remembered answered prayers and breakthroughs. There were jokes about the spooky late night terrorist-like prophesying that gave the youth a scared straight experience accompanied with tongues enhanced background sound effects. Also the times when soft angelic languages and gentle interpretations were spot on. As the gathering ended we prayed, tearfully hugged and parted company with a vow to keep.

Dear Tabla,
Had a hilarious time with dear friends talking about how we survived our childhood Spanish Pentecostal houses of worship ala Shawshank Redemption. I shared about elders Fela and Franco's toilet dispute. Gloria shared about her former extremely dogmatic pastor, who once was concerned about Raja's 'liberal' influence on the church's youth, sternly discouraged her from dressing modern and makeup. Dress and appearances were reinforced as unchanging biblical truths and senda antigua (ancient way) standard. That pastor herself, now decades later, sports dress pant suits, dyed cut short hairdos, makeup and jewelry while pastoring in a southern state based modern congregation. While laughing about this pastora outliving those poor females and males she and her spouse dogmatically exhorted, we also begrudgingly rejoice that she has been granted not to be devoured by past ignorances. Remembering his own excommunication from church due to the length of his hair, Ronnie suddenly began singing a song he heard in an old Hee Haw TV show:

"If you got long hair, there's sin your heart 2X
If your hair touch your ears there soon in your heart
And you can't get to heaven if there's sin in your heart
Chorus- Heaven yes, HELL NO!!! 3x
And you can't get to heaven if your hair is too long..."

The group also recalled the merchandising of rubber stamped healing cloths, made in China Holy Land trinkets, miraculous dental precious metal and porcelain fillings, and mysteriously appearing flowing oil on hands and walls. We grieved over the thousands of television sets deemed as one eyed demons and sledgehammered smashed asunder, now collectible vinyl record albums burned and gold crucifixes necklaces torn to pieces while singing Cristo Rompe Las Cadenas (Christ Breaks The Chains). We joked on how all those pieces of gold could have been melted down and sold to help fund deserving televangelists in need of air conditioned dog houses for their pampered pets. Also remembered:
Water dripping from the ceiling in the middle of a church service and the buckets that had to be placed to collect the water.
No heat in the middle of a wicked winter but still having to sit thru a service on hard wooden benches.
The chewed gum under the benches
Those silly banners on the walls.
Drum set (kids taking turns)
Food sale after service.
Walking up and down the church aisles collecting Avon or Stanley monies
.

Las maracas
Handheld Fans
Tambourine flying cymbals
The 2 hour long alter call.

Pulling down the gate and locking it down , when services was over.
Pastelitos late night after loooooooooooong service.
Selling food as a fundraiser (pro templo).
Giving out gospel tracts on busy streets.
Having lunch in the church basement on Sundays.
Pan caliente con mantequilla con queso y cafe (how buttered bread with cheese and coffee) - we had a bakery near our church.

We giggled and talked about how although tired, our moms always made sure we met Jesus. That being whenever they caught us misbehaving at our usual long weekday evening church services with chanclas named Jesus. Each of us told about other parents' disciplinary striking items, such as leather belts, belt buckles, electrical cords, and wire hangers which all were given biblical names. I then mindlessly asserted, like I had often heard from old timers, that parents today have become too soft. Then our conversation carelessly evolved into jesting on how we should patent and sell religious spanking paddles and rods. As we continued to joke and romanticized our past corporal punishing beatings, Milly just wore a sad smile. We hadn't seen her nor her super spiritual mother in ages. They had mysteriously moved away without notice to their friends, church family and neighbors. Milly then disclosed how years ago her mother gave her such a severe beating that it landed her in being hospitalized with a medically induced coma. The mother had back then rationalized, with the misuse of a nugget from eastern cultures of bible lands, that there were times when a good shepherd purposely broke a young sheep's leg to keep it safely close to him. Creating a bond between them as the mammal healed and became fond of the owner's heartbeat. Ultimately the sheep would not stray away from the flock. It's a popular illustration used by many preachers in their sermons, and tragically misapplied by some listeners. Milly asked us how was that toxic application, any different from religious terrorists killing their own rebellious children who stray away from their cultures and belief systems. Milly survived the physical assault and with much clinical and faith based therapy the mother detoxed from her abusive ways. We cried in sadness, cried in rejoicing that the mother and daughter survived the tragedy, and cried promising to be more prayerfully accountable for what is preached and taught in the Lord's name.

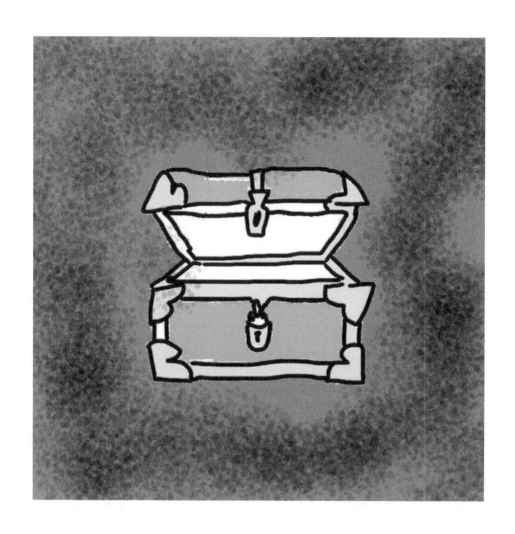

Treasures in Darkness

Be joyful in hope, patient in affliction, faithful in prayer.
Romans 12:12

Raja was looking through his journal, Tabla, reminiscing a lot about past experiences. He came across the time he lost a pastorate due to a scandal. It was a church that was thriving with new members. Many newly arrived immigrants were attracted to his Bible studies in their own language. Traditional churches they were raised in their country weren't very welcoming to them "here in America", or as they would say "here in the United States of America" – not America. The large traditional churches here in the states were not accommodating religious services and rituals in their language. They were fascinated and eager to inductively study and learn directly from the Scriptures as opposed to leaving Bible knowledge to clergy. They also wanted to study the Bible as a means to learn English. Then news broke out that Raja had engaged in a illicit sexual relationship years ago with a married woman resulting in a secret love child. Although Raja claimed that the news story was false, most of the congregants stopped attending the church. His wife Tesoro believed Raja and joined him in prayer and fasting. Years later, the pastor reads an entry recounting God's sustaining Grace.

"Dear Tabla, today I am happy yet broken. During the whirlwind of losing members, being called Wolf in Shepherd clothing and such I saw a bit of light. My wife saw a TV interview with the woman who claimed she had an illicit affair with me Tesoro taped the interview and dragged me to watch it. I finally got to see the woman slandering me standing next to her husband and the supposed Love Child. I became enraged and Tesoro laughed hysterically. We went to visit this family. When they answered the door they assumed we were reporters. I took out my small pocket writing pad and a pencil at which the sight of it prompted her to almost proudly identify herself as the woman in the news. She claimed

that it was a secret that she's been holding for many years and could not bear to hold it anymore. Her husband chimed in, indicating that he had forgiven her and supported her in making this public. A young lady came in behind him and said "I'm so glad mom finally told us. I really would like to meet my dad". I stared looked at the young lady and asked how old she was, to which she replied 19 years old. We looked at the parents who confirmed that the love child was 19 years old. Then like an angel of death my dear Tesoro Aideen Finley Harris Águila with her now fully inflamed Spanish Irish blood looked at them and said "May I make an introduction? My name is Tesoro and this is my husband Pastor Solomon Ojo De Águila who is 22 years old!!". As the threesome looked shocked, Tesoro continued "He must've been soooooome awesome lover at the age of only 3 years old, eh? By the way we are going to sue you for everything you've got". The husband looked at the woman and yelled "I told you we should have not listened to that priest!!" Later when the family retracted their slanderous claims, they disappeared from the community. Although my name was cleared most of the departed church members never returned. We ultimately had an empty rented sanctuary and eventually had no funds to remain there. Although Tesoro and I were grateful that we both were employed, I fell into an abyss of despondency. Tesoro called a old mentor of mine, asking for assistance in lifting my spirit. Reverend Heart came by and took me out to a diner near the Bible College he taught and inspired many students preparing for ministry. He listened intensely to my wounded heart as I shared doubts of my not being able to recover from this. Then he softly asked me to consider how joy and suffering can be twin coaches in our lives. Mentor Rev. Heart shared personal painful stories of losing three churches within a period of eight months due to unfair incidents. First church lost was when he didn't allow a popular speaker make unflattering innuendos regarding audience members of a particular culture. He told the audience that Rev. Heart threatened him against what the Holy Spirit had for the listeners that evening of great anticipation. Heart was ousted as pastor because he was stifling the work of the Spirit. Second church wanted Raja to exclude members in long term common law marriages with children from singing in the choir. Heart pointed out the hypocrisy of excluding them from contributing in choir ministry, yet wanting their tithes. Third church had an enthusiastic group of youth that had formed a musical band but the elders didn't want contemporary Christian music played. Heart compared the youth's contemporary music with the current church congo music once banned from their church which was now embraced by the elders. The elders became outraged accusing Heart of encouraging and promoting erogenous vulgar music. All three churches dismissed Heart, spreading defamatory tales against him. He fell into a deep depression that incapacitated him to the point he couldn't even watch baseball games and game shows on television. Whenever a game show contestant lost or a baseball player struck out, Heart would break down in tears. It was such a hard dark paralyzing time that he asked his in-laws that care for his wife and children for a time. Then Heart quoted the prophet Isaiah "I will give you the treasures of darkness, riches hidden in secret places, so that you may know that I am the LORD, the God of Israel, who summons you by name." There's a psychiatric hospital near Rev. Heart's home and church. Heart then told me "Who do you think that hospital calls when when they have a challenging case, particularly a patient who is a person of faith? They call me and those patients do well. I listen to them and help them through that dark valley....because I've been there... Because He has given me the experience of finding those hidden treasures and riches hidden in those darkness of despair". I from then on began to prayerfully perceive undeserved hardships with the filters of hidden treasures and twin coaches of joy and suffering.

Other Books by Author Jeffrey Cortez:

Peanut Butter
and a Little Extra Kindness

Authored & Illustrated by Jeffrey Cortez

Peanut Butter and a Little Extra Kindness

There were two boys that once in their lives suffered hunger. One day they were eating lunch. They each decided to share their half of their sandwich with someone they saw in need. They realized as they delivered the sandwich to the grateful person, that there were more people in need. When they got home they looked around the kitchen to see what extra things they had to share. Family, friends, and neighbors contributed from their spare possessions, time, and talents. The peanut butter sandwich became an abundant beginning of kindness. SPECIAL NOTE: The writers/illustrators royalties on this publication are donated to the New York City nonprofit that inspired the story (Manna of Life ministries, Bronx, New York)

Mantequilla de Maní y un Poquito de Bondad

Escrito y Ilustrado por Jeffrey Cortez

Mantequilla de Maní y un Poquito de Bondad

Habían dos niños que una vez en sus vidas sufrieron hambre. Un día estaban almorzando. Cada uno de ellos decidió compartir su mitad de su sándwich (torta) con una persona que vieron en necesidad. Al entregar el sándwich a la persona agradecida, se dieron cuenta de que había más personas necesitadas. Cuando llegaron a casa, miraron alrededor de la cocina para ver qué cosas adicionales tenían para compartir. La familia, los amigos y los vecinos contribuyeron con sus posesiones, sus tiempo y sus talentos. El sándwich de mantequilla de maní se convirtió en un abundante comienzo de bondad. Las ilustraciones en esta historia progresan lentamente desde dibujos lineales en blanco, negro y gris hasta dibujos totalmente coloreados que simbolizan la maravilla de la bondad colectiva. NOTA ESPECIAL: Las regalías de los escritores/ilustradores de esta publicación se donan a la organización sin fines de lucro de la ciudad de Nueva York que inspiró la historia (Manna of Life ministries , Bronx, Nueva York)

Grandma's Scribble Powers

Jeffrey Cortez
Sabbah,El-Roi & Abraham Ouedraogo

Grandma's Scribble Powers

Sofia told her grandmother that she was feeling frustrated and bored. Grandma tore a brown paper bag and began to scribble on it. The granddaughter began to learn how to use her imagination for fun and for problem-solving. No fancy and expensive tools needed. The story was inspired by the author's own memories of how his own 'abuela' would tear brown paper bags in order to entertain and teach me. An activity I now share with my own grandchildren and they with you readers. This book was created with my grandkids and their mom, my eldest, as models and assistant illustrators. We hope you enjoy it and go forth throughout your community and world with fun packed imagination and creative problem solving.

BooksbyJeffCortez@gmail.com